HUSH MONEY

The Cost of Being Black in Corporate America

Inspired by True Events

Deborah Harris, Jacquie Abram, and Delilah Harris

ISBN: 9798794901023

Cover Design by: Bookcover_pro

Editing & Formatting by: Deborah McDaniel

Printed in the United States of America by Kindle Direct Publishing

This book is dedicated to the matriarch of our family, a beautiful woman full of courage, faith, strength, and grace. We love you to the moon and back!

Contents

LIGHTNING NEVER STRIKES TWICE...RIGHT?

I NEVER KNEW THE COST OF BEING BLACK IN corporate America. The price I would pay with my dignity and fundamental rights as a human being just to have a job that wasn't in a low-income sector. A job that had a satisfying career path and gave me and my family a chance to live the American Dream. But if I knew then what I know now, maybe I would've done things differently before taking the job that traumatized and nearly destroyed me.

Maybe I would've bleached my dark skin to make it lighter or removed my long, Dookie braids to straighten my hair. Maybe I would've bought blue contacts to hide my brown eyes and got a nose job with a butt reduction, too—you know, do all the things I should've, would've, could've done to look less like me and more like *them* just to fit into a mold I had no part in creating.

No, I know me. And even if I could go back in time to that fateful day that changed my life in the worst way, I wouldn't change a thing 'cause I'm the strong, beautiful, Black woman God created me to be— dark skin, Dookie braids, big butt, and all. And although the last five years of my employment were horrific and I suffered in ways most people cannot imagine, that's all behind me now because I proved systemic racism in my workplace, kept my job, and was offered a six-figure settlement among other things.

3

And when I return to work after four weeks of paid vacation, I'll be confident that my career future will be better than my career past and excited that my battles against systemic racism in my workplace have finally come to an end. After all, lightning never strikes the same place twice...or so I thought.

If you haven't read the international best-selling prequel to this book *Hush Money: How One Woman Proved Systemic Racism in her Workplace and Kept her Job*, the authors strongly encourage you to read it first.

CHAPTER 1

A NEW LIFE FOR MOM

HAVE YOU EVER FELT SO HAPPY YOU THOUGHT YOU would burst? Or so excited you could barely contain yourself? I have. It was August 14, 2017, the day I signed the settlement agreement with my employer, Daebrun Career Institute, and reality sat in that in fourteen days I was going to receive a check for two hundred thousand dollars to settle the racial discrimination complaint I had filed with the state of Texas, compensate me for the emotional distress I suffered during my last five years of employment, and buy my silence. Two hundred thousand dollars—tax free! That's more money than I made in the last three years combined!

And words cannot describe how great it felt two days later when I drove away from that hell hole where I worked, the Temple campus, with my personal belongings in my trunk and thought about the huge financial blessing God was sending my way.

That's a lot of mula! I thought to myself as I gave the car a little gas and merged onto the highway to begin my commute back to my hometown of Austin, Texas. *What on earth am I gonna do with all that money?*

No sooner had I asked myself the question than I already knew the answer. The first and foremost thing I was going to do was give Mom the life she always deserved but never had. Mom. The woman who

5

adopted me when I was born and loved me unconditionally my entire life. The woman whose life was infinitely more precious to me than my own. The woman who was diagnosed with terminal colon cancer at the tender age of fifty-six and given one to two months to live by her doctor almost two weeks ago.

Mom was the most beautiful woman in the world to me with a taller than average height. And before she was diagnosed with colon cancer, she had a slender physique, caramel-colored skin as smooth as silk, glistening green eyes, and long shiny black hair. But months of chemo took a terrible toll on Mom and now she was a shadow of her former self with a thin physique, toffee colored skin as dry as desert sand, glassy green eyes, and almost no hair. But even so Mom was still the most beautiful woman in the world to me and living without her was simply not an option.

Mom never had a chance to live the American Dream not even when she was married to my adoptive father, King Marcus, a man who wasn't a king but who made me call him that anyway. King Marcus was a giant among mortal men. He was a handsome, high-yellow man with brown, clean-cut hair, hazel eyes, a boyish face, and a dazzling smile that melted mom's insides. He was so popular in our community that men wanted to be him, and women wanted to have him. But me—I feared him because beneath his suave, handsome, and debonair exterior was a monster who had a love of rum and a violent streak, usually ignited by the rum, that he regularly took out on mom. I couldn't have imagined in a million years back then that I would grow up and marry someone who was exactly the same.

My memories of King Marcus are spotty at best, but there is one thing I remember very well.

"You sure are ugly," he often said to me when Mom wasn't around with a smile on his face and a glass of rum in his hand.

On my fifth birthday, I decided to ask Mom the burning question that had been on my mind for far too long as she watched me coloring in my new coloring book.

"Did my other mommy not want me 'cause I'm ugly?"

Mom gasped.

"Absolutely not. Your other mommy thought ya' were as beautiful as I do. But she was sick and couldn't take care of ya'."

I stopped coloring to examine the orange crayon in my hand as the wheels in my head began to turn.

"Would I be prettier if I was orange like you and Gabby?" Gabrielle, my older sister by five years, was the biological daughter of King Marcus and Mom and at age ten she was mom's pre-cancer mini me with sun kissed skin, long jet-black hair, and mint green eyes.

Mom ran both hands through her silky hair to push it back. Then, she picked me up, put me on her lap, and moved a couple of my long box braids away from my face.

"Do you know why I named ya' Ebony?" She asked, looking deep into my brown eyes while caressing my cheek.

"No ma'am."

"I named ya' Ebony to highlight the beauty I see in you and your beautiful dark skin."

Mom's words were encouraging, but it was her gentle touch that comforted me the most as I looked into her beautiful green eyes and my cheek melted into the palm of her soft hand.

Mommy said I'm beautiful, I thought to myself as I beamed with pride on the inside.

Another thing I remember about King Marcus is that he was a good provider for our family despite his obvious flaws and the monster lurking inside him. And because of the income he earned working construction in the hotter months and as a garbage man during the colder months, our family lived quite well and was considered by many to be in Shreveport, Louisiana's upper class of poverty. We had a big mint green house with four bedrooms, a reliable car that looked great and ran great, too, an abundance of food on the table to eat, and even a television set in the living room.

Our lives drastically changed, though, when King Marcus abandoned us when I was just six years old. After that, it seemed like Mom was always hustling to keep us afloat. Don't get me wrong, Mom worked. She worked very hard as a waitress at the local pancake house.

But she made less than minimum wage, which, in 1990, was three dollars and eighty cents an hour plus tips...and that just wasn't enough. So, she hustled to make up the difference between what we had and what we needed and downgraded our quality of life to reduce expenses. For starters, we moved out of our big mint green house with four bedrooms into a small pink house near the railroad tracks that had three bedrooms and was infested with roaches. So many roaches. And they were *everywhere*. Here a roach. There a roach. Everywhere a roach-roach. And for some reason they loved Gabrielle's room—even though she kept it clean as a whistle—and we were convinced it was because they thought she was their leader.

King Marcus took our reliable car when he left, and our dignity and pride, too. So, Mom bought a new one. A red and brown station wagon that leaked green radiator fluid and had so many rust spots and dents that people in our neighborhood said our car had cellulite.

And as if losing our big home, reliable car, and dignity weren't bad enough—things were bad foodwise, too, and for the first six months after King Marcus left, there just wasn't enough to eat. So, Gabrielle and I regularly hopped our neighbor's fence when no one was home and helped ourselves to the green apples hanging on a tree in their backyard and the dog biscuits they kept in the milk delivery box on the front porch.

We lost everything we had because of King Marcus and didn't have much. But Mom was grateful for the little bit we did have and took us to church every Saturday to thank God.

Things got better after that, though, and there was plenty on the table to eat between the food we got from the church pantry; the crawdads and catfish Mom caught at the lake; the mystery meat that showed up in our kitchen sink every so often with its teeth, fur, and claws still intact that Mom swore was beef so we'd eat it, but I realized years later was opossum; and the food stamps. The dreaded rainbow-colored food stamps that might as well have been a big neon sign flashing LOOK AT US, WE'RE POOR as we stood in line at the grocery store checkout counter.

And when Gabrielle and I came of age and it was up to Mom as a single parent to have "the talk" with us about sex, she explained everything in a healthy and easy to understand way, ending the conversation with this: If you can't put salt and pepper on it, it does not belong in your mouth.

Mom sacrificed so much to take care of Gabrielle and me when it would've been easier to abandon us like King Marcus did. She worked hard year after year with no thought for herself and with no child support. She went to work on days when her body was so crippled with pain—she could barely move. And when the station wagon broke down—which it often did—she walked five miles to and from work, sometimes in blistering heat or torrential rainstorms, then soaked her swollen feet in Epsom salt to ease the pain so she could do it again the next day. And on days when food was scarce, she went without eating so Gabrielle and I could eat.

If there was anyone who deserved to live a better life it was mom. And I was willing to use every penny of my settlement money to make sure she did.

I made it back to Austin around 4 p.m. and went straight to mom's apartment. But as I reached for the door to open it, the hospice nurse, a kind gentle woman in her late sixties who reminded me of Mom in a lot of ways, opened it and walked out, saying goodbye to me in passing. Months ago, when mom's doctor informed us that her colon cancer had advanced from stage four to terminal, he recommended that we begin in-home hospice so that she could be as comfortable as possible in her own surroundings and start receiving end of life care. So, after getting in-home hospice setup, Gabrielle moved in with Mom and became her primary caregiver putting her life and career on hold so that I could continue fighting for my career at the Temple campus as racists tried to destroy it.

I walked in and saw Mom sitting on the couch watching TV with the tube from her portable oxygen tank in her nose and Aiyden, my eight-year-old son, sitting next to her. Aiyden was the miracle baby I thought I'd never have after three miscarriages—and a bad marriage—and grew to be the cutest little boy I ever saw with peanut colored skin, curly brown hair, and round hazel eyes.

9

"Mommy!" He yelled as he ran over and nearly knocked me down. "Can I play with your phone?"

Before I could answer, my little Houdini had reached into my purse, grabbed my phone, and was already playing a video game as he blindly walked back to the couch where Mom was adjusting the black wig she was wearing with her gloved hands. Mom started wearing gloves about three weeks ago because she developed peripheral neuropathy in her hands that was particularly painful when her bare skin was touched.

"Aiyden was grandma's good little boy," she said with a warm smile as I walked over and sat down next to her.

Gabrielle chuckled from the loveseat across from the couch.

"That's 'cause we let him play in the kitchen sink all day."

Gabrielle, who was now thirty-eight years old, was the spitting image of pre-cancer Mom in looks and in height. At six feet tall, she towered over my short self and still had sun kissed skin, long jet-black hair, and mint green eyes. But now she also had a figure that wouldn't quit, legs for miles, and a walk that could literally stop traffic.

Mom giggled at Gabrielle's remark as I walked over to the couch, kissed her on the cheek, and sat down next to her.

"I'm free!" I exclaimed with the biggest smile on my face.

Mom pumped her gloved fists in the air as the loose skin on her arms jiggled.

"You did it. I'm so proud of ya', honey. God is good!"

I carefully wrapped my arm around her frail body and leaned my head on her shoulder.

"Thanks, mom. I couldn't have done it without you."

Gabrielle loudly cleared her throat drawing attention to herself and causing Mom and me to laugh.

"And of course, I couldn't have done it without you either Gabby," I said to a giggling Gabrielle as she brushed her long hair. "We're two peas in a pod. A messed up, broke down, jacked up pod, but still a pod."

We all had a good laugh. Then I asked Mom the question that had been on my mind since the day I signed the settlement agreement.

"Mom, if we were rich instead of poor, what would our lives have looked like?"

"Ebony, I know what ya' thinkin'. You need to be smart and not blow all that money."

"Come on, mom," I protested. "We've been careful with money our whole lives 'cause we didn't have any and I'm on vacation, paid vacation, for the next four weeks. Can't we enjoy ourselves just once?"

"Hell yeah!" Gabrielle blurted out before Mom could respond.

"Language, Gabby!" Mom warned.

The room went silent. And as Mom sat quietly on the couch thinking, Gabrielle and I sat on pins and needles awaiting her response.

A few minutes later, Mom turned to me, and her tired eyes lit up like a Christmas tree in the dark.

"Okay." Mom smiled.

Gabrielle jumped up and did a happy dance as I clapped with glee.

"Yes!" I shouted. "Okay, so back to my question. What would our lives have been like if we weren't poor?"

Mom's eyes sparkled as she considered the possibilities and displayed a childlike sense of wonder. And for the first time in her adult life, she let her guard down, stopped worrying about anything and everything, and dared to dream.

"I suppose if we had money all those years ago, we never would've left Shreveport—our home. That's my biggest regret ya' know. Movin' us here isolated from our family and friends tryin' to find a better life for us that I never found."

For the next hour, I was covered in goosebumps as I listened to Mom sharing her deepest and innermost thoughts about the life she always wanted for us—the big house we would've lived in; the dinner parties full of Creole food we would've hosted; and the constant stream of love we would've received from family and friends. I listened

11

intently, silently thanking God for using me as the instrument to bless Mom and focusing on each word she spoke like a laser beam as I committed every detail to memory.

Afterwards, Aiyden and I went home where I warmed up leftovers for dinner and demanded Aiyden's stinky butt take a bath before I tucked him into bed. Under normal conditions I would've showered and gone to bed, too, but I was wide awake—too worried to sleep. *There's no way I can wait fourteen days for my money.* I thought to myself. *Mom may not have that long.*

I went to my room, sat down at my desk, and worried myself sick thinking about the possibility of Mom dying before I got my money, and she had a chance to live a better life.

Suddenly, I had an illuminating thought that gave me hope as I remembered a commercial I heard on the radio one day about a company that pays lump sums of cash to people who are expecting settlements but want their money fast. Excited, I turned on my laptop and did an online search, found a financial services company with good reviews and a good rating, and eagerly completed the online application.

The next morning as I was cooking oatmeal in my pink plushy bathrobe, my cell phone rang.

"This is Betty with Emerge N.C. Financial Services," a woman said with a scratchy voice. "Is this Ebony Ardoin?"

"Yes, it is."

"We received your application for purchase of your pending settlement, and I think we can help. I just need to ask you a few questions."

Over the next thirty minutes, I provided Betty with detailed information about me, the settlement I was expecting from Daebrun, mom's terminal cancer diagnosis and life expectancy, and contact information for my attorney and mom's doctor.

"Once we obtain the required documentation and verify everything, I'll email you the purchase agreement to sign."

"How long will it take for me to get my money after I sign the agreement?"

"About two days."

"Great, thank you!"

The next day, I received the purchase agreement from Betty via email stating that Emerge N.C. would purchase my pending settlement of two hundred thousand dollars for a fifteen percent transaction fee of thirty thousand. It also stated that the remaining amount would be issued to me in a lump sum payment via direct deposit into my bank account.

As you can imagine, I was beyond thrilled and immediately printed the agreement, signed it in front of a notary as instructed, and overnighted it back to Betty confident in the knowledge that within two days I would have the money needed for mom's better life to officially begin…or so I thought.

CHAPTER 2

THE HOUSE OF VIRGIE

FOUR DAYS HAD PASSED SINCE I OVERNIGHTED THE signed purchase agreement to Betty at Emerge N.C. and nothing had been deposited into my bank account. To make matters worse, it seemed that Betty was avoiding my calls because I left several urgent messages and had not received a single call back.

But early the next morning when I logged into my online bank account and discovered that I was one hundred seventy thousand dollars richer, everything changed. And because the funds were deposited electronically and cleared through the bank's Automated Clearing House, the entire amount was immediately available!

After screaming so loud that I woke Aiyden, and probably several neighbors, I called Gabrielle to share the good news as my hands trembled with excitement.

"I got the money, Gabby!"

"What? No way! Are you serious?"

"Yep, just got it!"

"But how? I thought you had to wait fourteen days."

"I paid thirty G's to get it now."

"Thirty G's? Damn, sis! We could've found a bootlegger and got it for half that price."

After hanging up the phone, I was as giddy as a schoolgirl as I skipped down the hall towards my bedroom to finally give Mom the life she deserved.

Seconds later, I arrived at my room and sat down on the edge of the bed.

Everything hinges on getting Mom back to Shreveport, I thought to myself.

A flight to Shreveport, Louisiana from Austin, Texas was about three hours, and I wasn't sure if Mom was physically able to make the flight, especially since she recently stopped chemo and began in-home hospice. So, I quickly grabbed my cell phone from the nightstand and called her doctor. Thankfully, he answered.

"Is Mom healthy enough to fly? I want to fly her to Shreveport for two weeks to be with family. It's about a three-hour flight."

"I don't see any reason why not," he replied, much to my surprise. "When you finalize the details, email them to me so we can setup hospice visits there."

After hanging up, I got to work searching the web for companies that offered the unique services I needed, making phone calls to get price quotes, electronically signing agreements to accept the arrangements, and wire transferring payments to finalize the details. And when I was finished four hours and two cups of coffee later, I leaned back in my chair, crossed my arms behind my head, and sat in total amazement at how fast the wheels of progress turn when you have a boatload of money.

Ecstatic, I called Gabrielle and could hear the happiness in her voice as I gave her all the details.

"Mom's gonna flip when she finds out!" She exclaimed.

"I know! We're on our way. Is she awake?"

"No, she's takin' a nap."

Twenty minutes later, Aiyden and I arrived at mom's apartment, opened the door, and saw Mom sound asleep on the couch. We went in as quietly as possible so as not to wake her, but when Aiyden saw Gabrielle sitting on the loveseat, he ran over to her.

"Aunt Gabby!" He screamed, jumping into her lap like an excited puppy. "Can I play with your phone?"

"How can I say no to that face?" She replied with a grin.

Mom, awaken by Aiyden's loud little mouth, slowly sat up on the couch.

"Oh man, I must've dozed off," she sleepily said. "How long ya' been here?"

"About five minutes," I replied, trying hard to contain myself.

I walked over to the couch, gave Mom a kiss on the cheek, and sat down next to her.

"We're going on vacation tomorrow, mom," I nonchalantly said.

"Oh, that's great honey," she replied, rubbing the sleep from her tired eyes. "You deserve a vacation after what ya' been through. Where are ya' going?"

"Not me, mom—we. *We* are flying to Shreveport in the morning."

Mom's tired eyes sprung open like a trap door.

"Did you just say we're—we're goin' home tomorrow?"

I smiled.

"Yes, me and Gabby are gonna get you packed."

"Oh, honey, that's too expensive. Let's wait 'til you get ya' money and then go."

"I already saved enough for our trip," I lied. "Don't worry mom, I got this."

Mom clasped her gloved hands together as tears of joy filled the bottom of her eyes.

"Thank ya', Jesus!" She cried out happily.

16

I gave Mom the address to our home away from home and instructed her to call everyone she knew in Shreveport to invite them to dinner tomorrow night.

After wiping the tears from her eyes and showering me and Gabrielle with hugs and kisses, Mom began calling every relative and friend she had in Shreveport to share the news. I got a ticklish feeling in my stomach as I watched Mom remove her glove and dial each number with an energy and enthusiasm I hadn't seen in a long time.

The next day, Aiyden and I arrived at mom's apartment at noon sharp, and I was happy to see that Mom was dressed and sitting in her wheelchair ready to go. And after the visiting hospice nurse gave Mom her medication and left, Gabrielle wheeled Mom outside with me and Aiyden following close behind with our luggage as we locked the apartment door and patiently waited near the curb for our ride.

"What time is the taxi picking us up?" Mom asked.

"Should be here soon," I replied casually.

A short time later, a shiny black limo driving in our direction caught mom's eye.

"Wonder where they're goin'," She randomly said.

You should've seen the look on mom's face a couple of minutes later when the limo pulled up and came to a complete stop in front of us. And when the chauffeur, who bared a striking resemblance to a young Smokey Robinson, walked over and opened the door in front of mom, she was smiling so big you could barely see her eyes.

"Your chariot awaits, Babette," he said in a deep sexy voice.

"Thank ya'!" Mom replied, turning to complete mush.

We eagerly jumped into the limo. And after the chauffeur put mom's wheelchair and our things in the trunk, we were off!

We drove for about twenty minutes until we arrived at a private airport in the heart of Austin and pulled up next to a stunning white jet with a perky flight attendant with long blonde hair and a short blue dress waving at us in the doorway.

"Welcome, Babette!" She enthusiastically shouted as we exited the limo, and the wind blew her hair.

Mom's eyes were as big as two glazed donuts.

"Th-That's our plane?" She stuttered.

"It sure is!" Gabby replied, adjusting her skinny jeans, and smiling like she had just won the lotto.

When we got out of the limo, Aiyden held my hand tight as he jumped up and down like an excited pogo stick. And after a minimally invasive security screening and assisting Mom with climbing the air step, we boarded the private jet, strapped into the oversized leather seats, and then we were off again!

Once we were airborne, we enjoyed a delicious lunch and were all impressed with the jet's amenities and comfort.

Three hours later, we landed at a small airport in Shreveport where another limo was waiting for us.

Mom sighed nostalgically as we exited the jet.

"We're home. We're finally—"

"Damn, it's hot!" Gabrielle screamed, interrupting mom's sentimental moment as a wave of scorching heat nearly knocked us over.

"Language Gabby!" Mom giggled. "Watch ya' language. It's hot in Austin, too."

"But not like this!" Gabrielle shrieked as a bead of sweat rolled down her forehead. "It's hot up in this mofo!"

There was absolutely no way I was going to jump in the middle of that conversation. But truth be known, I understood why Gabrielle reacted so strongly. It was nearly ninety degrees in Shreveport when we landed, and it was hot. Hot, humid, and sticky! And while Mom was having the time of her life floating around on cloud nine somewhere, the rest of us were sweating like pigs, swatting mosquitos left and right, and standing at the gates of Hell! Fortunately, it didn't take long to exit the aircraft and collect our things.

And after hopping into the air-conditioned limo and getting some much-needed relief from the heat, we were off again!

We drove through Shreveport for about fifteen minutes passing exit after exit as Mom eagerly looked out the window with eyes wide open. And when we approached the exit that leads to our old neighborhood, Mom had a smile on her face a mile wide.

"We're here!" She cried out, clapping her gloved hands with delight.

But when the chauffeur didn't take the exit she was expecting, she stopped clapping.

"We're not stayin' in our old neighborhood?"

"No, I got a deal on a place that's not too far away. We'll be there soon."

"Ok, honey."

Mom resumed looking out the window and a sly smile crept up my face. Fifteen minutes later, we took the exit to Ellerbe Woods, and when Mom realized where we were going her jaw literally dropped. Ellerbe Woods was a poor person's paradise with million-dollar mansions sitting on awe-inspiring estates. It was home to the richest of the rich in Shreveport and for two magical weeks, we would call it home.

"Oh my Lord," Mom softly said as we passed estate after luxurious estate. "If I'm dreamin' don't wake me. Let me sleep."

As we continued our journey through the land of the insanely wealthy, everyone in the limo was mesmerized, and it was so quiet you could hear a pin drop. That is, until we turned the corner and Mom caught a glimpse of the castle-like mansion with a *Welcome Babette!* sign spelled out in big decorative letters on the lawn.

Mom put both gloved hands on her cheeks and stared at the estate in astonishment.

"A mansion, child?" She asked as if she doubted her own eyes. "You got us a mansion?!"

I smiled.

The mansion was an impressive blend of medieval architecture and modern elegance with thirteen thousand square feet exquisitely designed with stone and adorned with turrets and crenellations. It was nestled on a magnificent multi-acre estate with beautifully landscaped grounds that included a colorful array of garden flowers and towering pine trees.

It also had a private lake as smooth as glass, a golf course rich in flora and fauna, an enclosed tennis court, and a resort-style swimming pool and patio. Even the circular driveway was grandiose in nature with a three-tiered marble fountain cascading crystal blue water in the center.

We pulled into the driveway and came to a complete stop in front of a butler, a chef, and twelve uniformed servants standing side by side in a line. And when the chauffeur retrieved mom's wheelchair from the trunk and assisted her as she emerged from the limo with her portable oxygen tank in hand, the servants warmly greeted her in unison.

"Welcome, Mademoiselle Babette!"

Mom sat in her wheelchair clapping her gloved hands and smiling completely consumed by the magic of the moment.

Seconds later, a tall pewter-haired man in his fifties with tan skin, grayish-blue eyes, and wearing a black and white butler's uniform proudly stepped forward carrying two dozen long stem roses.

"Mademoiselle Babette," he said with the dreamiest of French accents as he presented Mom with the roses. "I am Basile, and it is with greatest pride that we welcome you and your family to the House of Virgie."

"Thank ya' for havin' us," Mom replied, smelling the roses and smiling nonstop.

Basile escorted us through the sculpted double doors of the mansion, and we entered the entrance hall with mouths gaping wide. The entrance hall was bigger than my entire house! It had polished marble flooring with a plush red carpet running down the middle, three majestic golden thrones elevated by four marble steps at the carpet's end, large European oil paintings hanging on the walls, and Louis XV style tables and chairs full of hors d'oeuvres and drinks on both sides of the red carpet. But perhaps the most notable features of the entrance hall were the oversized crystal chandelier hanging in the center, the elevator made of glass and gold in one corner of the room, and the spiral staircase trimmed in pure gold on the other side.

Gabrielle bounced up and down, clapping her hands like a child on Christmas morning as Aiyden sporadically ran around the room. Then Basile gave us a tour of the House of Virgie which was remarkable and unlike anything we would ever hope to experience. From the lavishly furnished entertainment-sized rooms, extravagant bedroom suites, gourmet kitchen, and spectacular amenities, the House of Virgie was the Lamborghini of luxury retreats and absolutely perfect for my beautiful mom.

After the tour, we returned to the entrance hall where a delicious smelling aroma now filled the air.

"You girls smell that?" Mom gleefully asked. "Can't get that in Texas. That's Louisiana gumbo!"

Basile kneeled in front of Mom so they would be eye to eye as she sat in her wheelchair.

"Your dinner guests will be arriving soon, Babette," he said with a smile. "For the next two weeks, you are Queen of the House of Virgie. It's time to assume your rightful place."

Mom giggled.

"Okay, I'm ready."

Basile assisted Mom with getting out of her wheelchair, up the marble steps, and seated on the red velvet cushion of the golden throne in the center as Gabrielle and I sat on the smaller thrones located on each side. And as Aiyden played with his truck on the throne steps, Basile returned to the sculpted doors to greet mom's guest as they arrived while the rest of the servants stood side by side near him like they did earlier that day.

As we waited for mom's guests to arrive, my nerves were getting the best of me. I guess I just wanted everything to go off without a hitch to give Mom the special day she so richly deserved.

Suddenly, Basile made an announcement in a strong and stately voice for all to hear.

"May I present Madame Dottie Louise of the House of Walsh."

Seconds later, a plump woman with peach skin, sandy blonde hair, and chestnut brown eyes came barreling through the doorway and running down the red carpet towards us. And when Aiyden instinctively looked up and saw her heading our way with arms flailing, his eyes got as big as pancakes as he grabbed his truck and quickly moved out of her way.

"Babs, oh my God, Babs!" She cried out with a high-pitched voice as she ran up the throne steps and threw herself into mom's open arms.

"I'm so glad to see ya', my friend!" Mom softly said through tear-soaked eyes as she hugged her tight. "I didn't think I'd get here before I—,"

"Don't say it, Babs!" Dottie warned. "Don't even think it!"

Then, Mom introduced us to Dottie Walsh, her very best friend in the world, before the two of them started talking up a storm as Gabrielle and I watched with happy hearts.

Suddenly, Basile made another announcement in a strong and stately voice.

"May I present Monsieur Alexander Clay of—"

"You ain't got to announce me, Bruh," Uncle Alex said, casually waltzing through the door wearing sunglasses, a baseball cap, baggy blue jeans, and a Black Lives Matter shirt.

Uncle Alex, mom's younger brother, was fifty-two years old and quite the character. He was six foot three, athletically built with a broad chest, and had caramel-colored skin like Mom used to have, autumn green eyes, and graying brown hair.

When he entered the opulent entrance hall and saw Mom gracefully sitting on the throne at the far end, he whipped off his sunglasses and sprinted down the red carpet.

"Great googly-moogly!" He exclaimed, running up the throne steps and nudging Dottie out of the way before hugging Mom tight. "It's about time ya' came home, sis."

22

"I missed ya'," Mom replied as she got an unintentional whiff of cigarette smoke from his clothes. "X, are you still smokin'?"

Uncle Alex's eyes widened.

"Who me?"

"Don't play coy with me," Mom warned. "Your doctor said to stop smokin'."

"The thing of it is…you see—I'm quittin' tomorrow."

Mom giggled slightly.

"Liar."

Uncle Alex's clothes weren't the only things that reeked as Gabrielle soon discovered when he turned his attention to her.

"You were yay high the last time I saw ya', Neesey-Niece."

He made a knee-high gesture with his hand.

"I'm pretty sure I was taller than that Unc," Gabrielle laughed. "I was ten years old."

Uncle Alex reached his hand towards Gabrielle's ear and leaned in close.

"I found a quarter in your ear, Neesey-Niece," he said with breath that smelled like a toxic combination of smoke, beer, and gingivitis.

Gabrielle gave him a fake laugh as he showed her the quarter in his hand, followed by a pitter patter hug.

"It's great to see ya', Unc," she said. "Go pull a quarter from Eb's ear before she gets jealous."

As Uncle Alex headed my way, Gabrielle quietly giggled as I shot darts at her with my eyes.

Uncle Alex gave me a big bear hug and whispered in my ear with dragon breath that nearly melted it.

"You got a money tree ya' hidin' somewhere Neesey-Niece?".

"Leave that child alone, X," Mom warned.

23

"Alright. Alright. But word on the street is Eb here won the lotto. I just wanna give her some fatherly advice."

Uncle Alex grabbed my hand and looked deep into my eyes.

"Eb, God gave ya' a head and an ass. If you don't use ya' head, ya' might as well have two asses."

I gently yanked my hand from his grasp and stared at him dumbfoundedly.

"Umm—thanks for those pearls of wisdom, Unc."

Over the next fifteen minutes, aunts, cousins, and five more of mom's friends arrived, each one walking or running down the red carpet to greet mom. Thankfully, some brought kids who immediately started playing with Aiyden and kept him occupied.

Watching Mom bask in the love of people she hadn't seen in decades was priceless and had me and Gabrielle smiling so big that our cheeks hurt. With Mom being the happiest she'd been in a very long time, I knew that using my settlement money to make her dreams come true was the right decision and nothing or no one could kill her joy...or so I thought.

CHAPTER 3

THE VAMPIRE

THE ENTRANCE HALL WAS ALIVE WITH JUBILANCE AS folks snacked on finger foods and laughed, cried, and sometimes did both while showering Mom with love amidst the thick scent of tantalizing food in the air. And when the chef came in and invited everyone to the dining room for dinner, the group resembled a stampede as they eagerly followed him out.

With all of mom's guest in the dining room, Basile instructed the servants to return to their respective stations as he closed the sculpted doors and proceeded to walk down the red carpet to assist us with mom. Suddenly, the doorbell rang causing him to turn around and briskly walk back.

A few moments later, he made one more announcement in a strong and stately voice.

"May I present King Marcus of the House of Ardoin."

"King Marcus?" Gabrielle gasped, turning to me in horror.

Don't invite the vampire into the house, Basile! I screamed in my head, unable to form words.

But it was too late.

25

The vampire had already swaggered through the door wearing a sleek pinstriped suit and was heading down the red carpet towards us in what appeared to be slow motion. King Marcus. The man night terrors were made of.

The man who submerged mom's beautiful face in a sink full of dishwater and nearly drowned her in front of Gabrielle and me.

The man who choked Gabrielle with his leather belt for trying to help mom.

The man who threw me against the wall for trying to help Gabrielle.

As he made his way to the throne steps acting like the cock of the walk, I felt sick to my stomach as a wave of repressed memories hit me like a tsunami.

"You look beautiful, Bae," King Marcus said, flashing Mom the smile that once melted her insides as he walked up the throne steps, leaned down, and attempted to give her a kiss on the cheek.

Thankfully, Gabrielle sprang into action like a superhero putting her hand between mom's cheek and his lips.

"Mothafucka, please!" She yelled.

"Is that any way to talk to ya' daddy, girl?"

"Daddy! Why you sorry sack of sun-dried rat shit—"

"Language, Gabby," Mom calmly said, interrupting her rant.

King Marcus stood back up and narrowed his eyes at Gabrielle before refocusing his attention on mom.

"Is there some place private we can talk, Bae?" He gently asked.

"No. Whatever ya' came here to say, ya' gonna have to say right here."

King Marcus cleared his throat, got down on one knee, and grabbed mom's gloved hand.

"You were the best part of me, Bae," he continued as Gabrielle and I rolled our eyes in disgust. "And I never should've left. But I'm here now and I want ya' back."

I jumped into the conversation after the shock of seeing him wore off. "People in hell want ice water, too," I said, as smug as I could be.

"Ebony, that's enough," Mom interjected. "I can speak for myself."

I know Mom wanted me to stop but taking King Marcus on after all those years of fearing him had me so high on adrenaline that I couldn't. So, I continued.

"And we know exactly why you're here. So, to be clear, *King Marcus*, you're not getting one dime from us! Not one dime! So, get the hell away from our mom!"

King Marcus stood back up as his face contorted with rage.

"Your mom!" He laughed. "Before she was your momma, girl, she was my wife and I told her I didn't want ya' blackity black ass. Nobody wants ya'. I don't want ya'. Ya' real momma didn't want ya'. And from what I hear, ya' husband don't want ya' either. No amount of money in the world changes that!"

"Marcus! Stop!" Mom screamed as Basile sprinted across the room to help.

His words cut me deep and left me speechless, as another repressed memory from my childhood hit me in the face like a sledgehammer.

It was Christmas morning, and I was four years old. Gabby and I eagerly ran into our living room to open our gifts. One by one, we opened the few we had. When they were all opened, King Marcus opened our coat closet and pulled out two more gifts—dolls he purchased. For Gabby, King Marcus bought a beautiful blonde-haired Barbie with multiple accessories. But for me...he bought a Black Raggedy Ann.

I didn't understand the significance of his gifts at the time because I was just grateful to receive a doll. But now, at thirty-three, with him standing in front of me spewing hate and foaming at the mouth like a rabid dog—I understood. Those dolls weren't mere toys.

They represented how he felt about Gabrielle and me and I finally understood why he treated me like some kind of mutant my entire life.

King Marcus was a Black man who couldn't accept me as his child because of my dark skin—something I later discovered is called Colorism—and that made him just as bad as the racists as far as I was concerned.

"Monsieur, I'm afraid I have to ask you to leave," Basile urged, grabbing King Marcus' arm to escort him out.

"You don't have to ask me *nothin'*!" He yelled, forcefully yanking his arm from Basile's grasp.

King Marcus adjusted his suit jacket, winked at me, and donned a devilish grin as he turned to walk away.

"Marcus, wait," Mom said with the sweetest of voices as she shakily pushed herself up from the throne to stand.

"Don't leave, baby."

Gabrielle and I stood with jaws dropped as Mom carefully removed the glove from her right hand while King Marcus climbed the throne steps.

"I knew there was still love between us, Bae," he whispered, looking deep into mom's beautiful green eyes.

Suddenly, Mom used every ounce of strength she had to slap him so hard that spit flew out of his mouth.

"Your wrong!" She cried out. "And if you ever come near me or mine again, I'll use that money we got to make ya' disappear— permanently. Now get the hell out of my house 'cause *I'm the queen* of the House of Virgie and I don't need a king."

King Marcus was stunned and as he walked away with Basile on his tail and the sting of mom's handprint still on his cheek, Gabrielle and I clapped our hands and cheered.

"Is your hand okay, mom?" Gabrielle asked, helping Mom sit back down on the throne and putting her glove on.

"It hurts a lot, but it was worth it. You girls okay?"

After confirming that we were okay we shared a group hug, and it was a great way to end that chapter of our lives.

We got Mom situated in her wheelchair shortly thereafter and followed Basile into the formal dining room where mom's guests and my son were anxiously waiting. The dining room wasn't nearly as large as the entrance hall but was still impressive with glowing wall sconces, a large picture window with a spectacular view of the estate, a wall-sized marble fireplace creating ambiance and warmth, and a collection of high-end mahogany furniture steeped in European elegance.

"Sit next to me, Babs!" Dottie yelled from the long rectangle table in the center of the room.

The table, exquisitely designed with hand carvings throughout, was beautifully laid with white porcelain china, cobalt blue goblets, and the most scrumptious-looking food we couldn't wait to taste—Cajun fried catfish with Creole mustard and gumbo with smoked sausage, shrimp, and chicken; steamed rice, sweet cornbread, and fried okra for our sides; and Bananas Foster cheesecake, New Orleans-style beignets, and banana bread pudding for our desserts.

When Mom saw all her favorite foods spread out on the table, her mouth began to water for the first time since chemo caused a loss in appetite. And after Mom spent several minutes thanking God in the name of Jesus for family, friends, food, and fellowship, we got our grub on and for the next hour and a half all you could hear were forks clanging on plates, chewing sounds from all directions, and multiple conversations happening all at once as we shared details of our encounter with King Marcus.

"He's lucky I wasn't there," Uncle Alex said, weighing in on the conversation. "I would've knocked his lanky ass down a few pegs."

Dottie glared at him with eyebrows raised from across the table.

"But how did he know Babs was here?"

Uncle Alex nervously looked the other way to avoid Dottie's unblinking gaze as everyone at the table fell silent awaiting his response.

"Well?" She asked with arms crossed, rapidly tapping her foot on the floor.

Uncle Alex didn't say a word. He just looked around the room avoiding eye contact.

"Alex!" Dottie screamed, startling him.

"Shut ya' pie hole, Dot." He finally answered.

Mom jumped into the conversation looking at him with side eyes. "X, did you have a hand in Marcus showin' up here?"

He swallowed hard.

"The thing of it is you see, I may of possibly—uh, I mean you know kind of in—in a roundabout way as it were, said somethin' to his lanky ass 'bout y'all gettin' a million dollars and a mansion in Ellerbe Woods."

"A million dollars?" Mom shook her head in disgust. "X, how could ya'? How could ya' do that to me—to my girls?"

Uncle Alex's head dropped in shame as he looked down at the table.

"I'm sorry, sis. I didn't mean to hurt ya'. I just wanted to rub his highfalutin' nose in it. I knew he'd show up when I gave him the address, I just thought I'd be there to kick his ass when he did, that's all."

"Highfalutin', Alex?" Dottie mockingly asked. "That's the best word you could come up with?"

The table erupted in laughter lightening the mood as Mom gave Uncle Alex a warm smile.

"I forgive ya'," she said. "You know I never could hold a grudge."

After dinner ended, mom's guests left but most of them returned with overnight bags to spend as much time with Mom as possible and live in the lap of luxury for the duration of our stay.

Mom was completely worn out after dinner and began experiencing cramping in her stomach. So, a female servant escorted us to the luxurious master bedroom suite on the second floor using the gold and glass elevator in the entrance hall.

30

And as I gave Mom a sponge bath and tucked her into bed, Gabrielle called the hospice agency to report her pain and provide detailed information like when it started, where it was, and how long it lasted.

Fifteen minutes later, a hospice nurse stopped by and as I tucked Aiyden into the extra bed across the room that was added per my request, she checked mom's vitals and gave her a higher dose of morphine to manage her pain through the night before leaving.

Gabrielle kissed Mom goodnight and went to her suite to relax and unwind. And me? I climbed into bed with Mom the way I did all those years ago when I was struggling financially and living with her in her small one-bedroom apartment.

Mom's head sank into the pillow.

"I don't know how ya' did it child," she blissfully said. "But thank you. Thank you for bringin' me home & doin' all this for me."

I smiled and kissed her on the cheek.

"I'm going to use the rest of my settlement money to get you the best doctors money can buy. Ones that'll be more aggressive and—"

"No, Ebony," Mom softly objected. "I love ya', but no."

"But mom—"

"I'm not gonna let ya' waste ya' money tryin' to change God's will. The only thin' another doctor will do is make ya' go broke."

"You don't know that mom."

"Yes, I do. All they'll do is pump more poison in me and I'm not goin' through that again. Last chemo turned me into the crypt keeper. Sometimes I wish I never got it."

"Don't say that mom, you're beautiful as ever."

Mom slightly giggled as the morphine started to take effect.

"Liar," she softly said as her words began to slur. "Listen honey. I want to spend the time I have left with you kids, not on chemo. "You did somethin' wonderful for me. Do somethin' wonderful for you. Understand?"

31

A single tear rolled down her cheek as she closed her eyes and gave in to the sweet relief of sleep.

"Okay, mom," I whispered, kissing her on the forehead. "I love you."

Words cannot express how difficult it was to hear Mom say that she was done fighting for her life. And, I'll be honest, part of me wanted to hire doctors anyway to force her to fight because I couldn't bear the thought of spending a single minute living a life without Mom in it to comfort me, guide me, and help me raise Aiyden.

But the other part of me, the part that loved and respected Mom with all my heart, overruled knowing that it was her decision to make not mine. And because Mom believed the Apostle Paul when he said to be absent from the body is to be present with the Lord, I believed him, too.

The remainder of our vacation was just as magical as the first day. Mom's family and friends spent precious time with us and enjoyed our vacation getaway as they laid by the pool on the resort style patio, enjoyed the most delectable Creole food, and watched movies in the magnificent home theatre. And although our lifestyle of the rich and famous only lasted two weeks, the love Mom received during that time and the memories she made were a lifetime's worth.

On our last day at the House of Virgie, Basile gave Mom a warm hug.

"I'll miss you, Babette," he said with a smile. "You are my favorite Queen."

"I'll miss you, too, my friend."

As we drove to the airport for our flight home and Ellerbe Woods became a distant memory, I looked forward to my first day as the National Director of Student Finance and was confident I would receive a better level of training than I had the last time I was promoted…or so I thought.

CHAPTER 4

THINGS AREN'T AS THEY SEEM

WE RETURNED TO AUSTIN, TEXAS THE SAME WAY WE left, and I spent the last week of my vacation moving Mom and Gabrielle into the bi-level house I was renting and buying new furniture to accommodate their stay, gifting Gabrielle thirty thousand dollars for being the best daughter to Mom and sister to me that we could ever ask for, and buying Aiyden his very own cell phone to play all the games he loved. I also took Mom's advice and bought two things just for me: a showroom new, candy apple red Ford Mustang and a new wardrobe that flattered my figure because let's face it, I gained weight. And at five-foot-four there was a lot more of me to love. But there were also curves. Curves for days. And I wanted to accentuate those curves.

On the morning of September 18, 2017, while Mom and Gabrielle were still asleep, I got dressed for work, kissed Aiyden on the forehead before he boarded the school bus, and drove to work enjoying the power of my new muscle car and that new car smell. At that moment, I felt pretty good. Mom's health wasn't showing any signs of decline which I took as a positive and I was actually looking forward to starting my new job as the National Director of Student Finance.

I would never admit this to anyone, but I desperately needed a break from worrying about Mom because it hurt so much and was killing me slowly. And I felt guilty for needing a break. Was it wrong of me to want a moment to focus on something else—anything else?

As I continued driving, I listened to a song called *Like the Moon* by Future Island and felt a peace and a calm that I hadn't felt in a really long time. That is, until a flashback of King Marcus at the House of Virgie caused my self-esteem to plummet.

I told her I didn't want ya' Blackity Black ass. Nobody wants ya'. I don't want ya'. ya' real momma didn't want ya'. And from what I hear ya' husband don't want ya' either.

I pushed the clutch with my foot and angrily shifted gears.

Great. Just great. Rejected by Blacks, hated by Whites. Where do I belong?

Fifteen minutes later, I pulled into the parking lot of Daebrun Career Institute's Austin campus. And as I walked through the front door wearing a blue silk skirt suit, two-inch high black pumps, and gold hoop earrings to complement my braids, I was a vision of confidence—on the outside, that is. On the inside, I was a basket case as King Marcus' words haunted me like a poltergeist.

I walked up to the reception desk and was greeted by a freckled faced woman in her early twenties with short red hair, a nasally voice, and a thousand-watt smile.

"Good morning, welcome to Daebrun."

"Good morning. I'm Ebony Ardoin, the National Director of Student Finance."

"Great, I'll let Cody know you're here. Please have a seat."

"Who's Cody?"

"The Director of IT,"

I sat down in the lobby as instructed to wait for Cody. But as I glanced around the campus where my decent into Hell initially began, I realized the wounds from racism were still fresh. And as I recalled the chilling words from Dr. Taylor, the racist Chancellor and she-devil at the Temple campus, I began to panic.

> *"I'm just trying to help you,"* Dr. Taylor said. *"You left Austin to get away from the wolves, right?"*
>
> *"True. And since you know that I'm sure you also know that the wolves I had problems with are gone now."*
>
> *Dr. Taylor locked eyes with me, leaned forward, and whispered something that sent an eerie chill down my spine. "But their pups are still there, and they're very hungry."*

Flustered, I closed my eyes and inhaled deeply. *Get it together, Ebony,* I told myself, deciding at that moment that I was going to start my new job hoping for the best, but planning for the worst just in case there was any truth to Dr. Taylor's warning.

I slowly exhaled and when I opened my eyes, I noticed him. A ruggedly handsome man walking towards me wearing Levi jeans and a beige polo shirt with Daebrun's logo on it. He was well over six feet tall and athletically built with warm vanilla skin, sandy blonde crew cut hair, crystal blue eyes, and a chiseled chin with no facial hair.

As he got closer, I stood up to greet him.

"Hey, Ebony," he said with a smooth voice as he walked up and offered his hand to me. "I'm Cody, the Director of IT."

I shook his hand, looking up to make eye contact as he towered over me.

"It's nice to meet you, Cody."

"Likewise. You worked here before, right?"

"Yes, five years ago."

"Well, I'll give you a tour any way, then take you to your office. It's in Building 2."

"Thanks, I appreciate that."

"No worries, I'm easy for you."

Cody was likable and resembled the Russian fighter in that movie *Rocky*. And as we walked through Building 1 and made small talk about the weather and other trivial things, I found myself enjoying his company and it seemed that he was enjoying mine, too. And even though nothing in Building 1 had changed over the last five years except the carpet and wall paint, it was nice being welcomed by a friendly face after everything I had endured with racists there.

A short time later, we exited Building 1 and entered the campus courtyard where the fragrant scent of noisette roses delighted my senses. I had forgotten how beautiful the courtyard was with its lush green grass, trees full of autumn red leaves, shrubs and rose bushes abound, and cobblestone walkways. And as Cody and I enjoyed the beauty of our surroundings while we walked and talked, the anxiety I felt earlier that day melted away. Things were great so far, and I knew they had the potential to stay that way well beyond day one.

Cody and I completed our walk through the courtyard and arrived at Building 2 about seven minutes later. Building 2 housed Daebrun's CEO, executive leadership team, and national directors who, like me, were one level higher than campus directors and staff in the organizational hierarchy and were responsible for providing training, oversight, and resources to their respective departments at all campuses in the Daebrun division.

When Cody unlocked the door, we went inside, and subsequently triggered the building's alarm, which began making a series of warning beeps. After punching the code into the keypad near the door to disarm the alarm, he turned on the lights.

"Where is everyone?" I asked, glancing around the building in astonishment.

"At Corporate for some kind of bigwig conference."

"Why aren't you there? Aren't you a bigwig?"

"No, not exactly. I'm what you might call a glorified grunt. I'm campus IT but I take care of all buildings."

"Well, when do the bigwigs get back?"

"Friday."

Friday was four days away and the thought of having the entire building to myself to settle in appealed to me. But as I continued glancing around, I became increasingly disappointed with the layout of Building 2 because it left a lot to be desired. It was small in comparison to Building 1 and the longer I stayed the more I missed the hustle and bustle of campus life. There were no students loitering the halls excited about the weekend. No faculty teaching classrooms alive with energy. No staff running to and from the breakroom. Just offices. Lots of offices and a conference room, breakroom, and two bathrooms.

Cody escorted me to my office in the far-left corner of the building and as we walked, I was prepared to be equally unimpressed. But when he unlocked the door and moved aside like a true gentleman letting me enter first, I froze in the doorway as my jaw literally dropped. I couldn't believe my eyes.

My office wasn't unimpressive at all, it was perfect! Better than perfect! It was spacious with natural light and beautifully decorated with matching cherry wood furniture including an L-shaped executive desk to the right, a filing cabinet with two wide drawers opposite the door, and a five-shelf bookcase with a bamboo palm plant to the left. But of all the features that set my office apart from the drabness of Building 2, my favorites were the abstract paintings hanging on the walls and the large window over the filing cabinet with a great view of the campus courtyard.

As I continued standing in the doorway and marveling at my new office, I totally forgot about Cody who had quietly moved in close behind me.

"You gonna stand in the doorway all day?" He playfully laughed, startling me.

I quickly turned around to give him a witty response but was thrown off my game by the bulge in his jeans that caught my attention. *Is he hard?* I asked myself, staring intensely as so many questions raced through my mind. *Why didn't I see that earlier? Was it there the whole time?*

Suddenly, it dawned on me that I was still staring at it! Mortified, I looked down trying to play it off hoping by some miracle that he didn't notice me staring. But when I slowly lifted my head up and made eye contact with him, he was grinning at me like the cat that ate the canary and there was no doubt in my mind—he noticed. I began to blush.

Embarrassed and a little freaked out, I turned around to break his gaze, briskly walked inside my office, and nervously sat down in the chair behind my desk.

Cody walked in and stood in front of my desk *still hard,* mind you, and staring at me with smoldering eyes.

"Is there anything else you need, Ebony?"

"No. I-I'm good. Uh—I mean yes. Yes. I need keys."

He smiled as he reached into his pocket and pulled out a set of keys and a card containing instructions for setting the building alarm. And when he reached over the desk to give them to me and his hand slightly grazed mine, the butterflies in my stomach began to flutter.

"You gonna be okay here by yourself?" He asked. "I can check on you later if you want."

"No, that's not necessary. But thank you for asking."

He smiled.

"No worries. I'm easy for you."

And with that he turned and walked away, and I was left sitting in my office alone and speechless.

Cody was a tall drink of water who could probably have any White woman on campus he wanted. But maybe, just maybe, King Marcus was wrong when he said nobody wanted me. Maybe, against all odds, Cody wanted me.

I didn't know.

But one thing I did know with one hundred percent certainty is that Cody was one of *them* and not to be trusted. And even if he did call himself flirting with me, he was wasting his time because after everything I had endured with racists at Daebrun, there was absolutely no way on God's green earth that I would ever be romantically or physically interested in a White man.

After Cody left, I created the first weapon that I would use to protect myself and defend my career if racism still existed at the Austin campus—my Daily Log. My Daily Log was a document I used to keep track of conversations and important events as they occurred and was very effective the last time I fought racism at the Temple campus. And because I still wasn't comfortable using my smart phone to secretly record conversations, even though I knew that Texas was a one-party consent state and federal law approved of secretly recording conversations you are a party to, I still worried about getting caught.

After logging into my computer, I opened a new document, named it Daily Log, and inserted a three-column table with Date, Time, and Description headers. Then, I made my first entry in my Daily Log and saved it on the same free online cloud storage website I found on the internet the last time I fought racism for safekeeping.

DAILY LOG

Date	Time	Description
9/18/17	9:00 a.m.	Arrived at the Austin Campus to start my new job as National Director of Student Finance. I was greeted by Cody, the Campus Director of I.T. and escorted to my office in Building 2. No one was there, they were all at a bigwig conference.

After my Daily Log was created and saved, I decided to put the embarrassing ordeal with Cody behind me and focus on learning every aspect of my new job to ensure my success. The problem with this plan, though, was that no one was available to mentor me, guide me, or even do something as basic as provide me with my job description. I literally started my new job with nothing.

No training, no resources, no tools, and no information about how to successfully perform it. And because I didn't want to waste precious time twiddling my thumbs while I waited for the "bigwigs" to return, I kept myself busy doing things that came natural to me.

I ran reports to assess operations at each campus, reviewed prior year audit results to determine weaknesses and identified opportunities for training and growth.

Then, I scheduled video conferences with each Student Finance team so I could build rapport.

I also found a National Director of Student Finance job description on the internet to get an idea of what my new job entailed and reached out to people in my predecessor's rolodex to introduce myself and create my own resources.

The next day, after wrapping up a video conference, Cody stopped by.

"Hey, just checking on you. Any issues with your phone or computer?"

"No, everything's working fine."

"I'm going across the street to get some grub. Want me to bring you something?"

"No, I brought my own lunch but thanks for asking."

"No worries, I'm easy for you."

Immediately after Cody left, I immersed myself in work doing everything I could to get a handle on my new position and set myself up for success.

The next day I arrived at work bright and early and when I walked into my office, I was pleasantly surprised by the delicious aroma in the air. And when I saw the large cup of joe on my desk along with a cheese bagel and a chocolate chip cookie, I donned a big smile. It was the nicest thing anyone had done for me in a very long time, and I knew just who to thank. But before I had a chance, my desk phone rang. It was Cody.

"Top of the mornin' to you, Ebony."

I giggled. "Top of the mornin' to you."

"Like your surprise?"

"Yes, very much. You are too kind."

40

"Nah, I'm just easy for you."

I giggled again.

"Well, thank you for being easy for me."

He chuckled and quickly hung up, and as I sat at my desk sipping coffee, I found myself daydreaming, as thoughts of Cody invaded my mind.

Suddenly, I realized what I was doing and quickly shook my head to snap out of it. *Why am I thinking about that man? He's not my type.*

I put down the coffee, logged into my computer, and tried to get lost in the mountain of unread email that had accumulated over the last four weeks to take my mind off Cody. But every time I paused even for a minute, my mind wandered back to him and, embarrassing to say, his hard-on.

What's wrong with you? He's White for goodness sake!

You can't be attracted to Cody, he's not even your type!

Truth is, I really didn't know what my type was. I got married right out of high school to a military man turned abusive husband not because I was in love but because I didn't think I could do any better. You see, unlike my beautiful big sister Gabrielle who had boys falling all over her when we were kids and men begging to drink her bathwater when we grew up, I was socially awkward with low self-esteem—which I blamed entirely on King Marcus—and felt much like the Black Raggedy Ann doll he gave me. And after my disaster of a marriage ended, I wasn't ready to trust another man with my body or my heart. So, there was no way I could be attracted to Cody because, to be honest, I still wasn't ready to trust anyone, but especially a White man.

For the next two and a half hours, I did everything I could to stop thinking about Cody. I read more emails. I ran reports. I made calls. But in the end, I always found myself staring aimlessly at the wall thinking about his fine ass and the part of me that wanted to give in to reckless abandon to satisfy the desires that were building inside me.

But the other part of me, the more logical part, overruled. And since it was clear that I wasn't going to get any amount of work done until I dealt with the horny elephant in the room, I called Gabrielle..

41

"C'mon Eb. You seriously can't see what's goin' on here?"

"Yeah, I do. Cody wants some chocolate and I'm trying really hard not to give it to him."

"Listen, sis. I know it's been years since anyone tapped that ass. And I know it's temptin', but get ya' mind outta the gutter for a minute. Don't you think it's odd that on the day you return to work, this fine specimen of a man—who don't even work in the same building with ya'—just comes to collect ya'? And everybody just happens to be gone, leaving y'all alone while he's walking around with a hard-on?"

"It does sound odd now that you mentioned it."

"Eb, I can tell you like this guy, but I don't trust him. I think they're setting ya' up again and you're making it waaaay too easy. Last time they said you were harassing that other good looking White guy. What was his name?"

"Michael—"

"—Right. And now they're settin' ya' up for sexually harassing this one."

When Gabrielle brought up Michael, I thought I was going to be sick. Michael was that racist spawn of Satan and my former employee at the Temple campus who teamed up with Dr. Taylor, the racist Chancellor, to have me falsely investigated for harassment to derail my career and steal my job.

Still, even with all that, I wasn't quite ready to concede, so I made one final attempt to debunk Gabrielle's theory.

"But what about the hard-on, Gabby?" I asked. "You know as well as I do, no man can fake a hard-on."

"I don't believe for a second he was hard. He probably stuffed a balled-up sock in his pants when ya' weren't lookin'."

After hanging up with Gabrielle, I felt like a complete jackass. She was right. I was being set up again and they were using Cody to do it this time!

For the next fifteen minutes, I documented everything that happened with Cody in my Daily Log and beat myself up for being so damn gullible. Then, I grabbed my purse and keys, closed my office door, and headed towards the exit to go home for lunch to lick my wounds. But before I made it to the door, in walked Judas—Uh, I mean Cody.

"Hey, Ebony, wanna grab some lunch?"

"No," I curtly said.

"There's a great Korean restaurant across the street. I'll buy."

"No thank you. I'm going home for lunch."

"Go home tomorrow. Have lunch with me."

Annoyed, I snapped.

"Don't you have a computer somewhere you could be fixing, man? You're always saying you're easy for me. Go be easy for someone else!"

Cody—clearly taken aback by my anger—sharply inhaled like he wanted to say something. But instead, he lowered his head and shook it, quickly turned around, and quietly walked out.

And by this point, I was too upset to eat anything, so I returned to my office and slumped in my chair as my eyes teared up. I wanted so desperately to believe that King Marcus was wrong. That there *was* someone who wanted me. And not just someone, Cody. I don't know if you can understand how I felt, but I think Malcolm X described my feelings perfectly when he said:

"The most disrespected person in America is the black woman. The most unprotected person in America is the black woman. The most neglected person in America is the black woman."

And after a lifetime of rejection, I truly believed the most rejected person in America was *this* Black woman—me.

So, thinking that a gorgeous White man was attracted to me after years of being disrespected, unprotected, neglected, and rejected…well, it validated me somehow and made me feel beautiful for the first time in my life.

43

But now, sitting in my office, it hurt like hell to discover that his interest in me was just another ruse and that I was being setup again by Daebrun. Depressed couldn't even begin to describe the feeling.

Cody avoided me for the rest of the day and the following day, too, and I was just fine with that. I wanted nothing to do with him and I was sure the feeling was mutual…or so I thought.

CHAPTER 5

CHOCOLATE & VANILLA SWIRL

THE NEXT DAY, DR. HARRY GERSHON AND THE OTHER "bigwigs" returned from the conference and the population in Building 2 increased by a whopping ten. Dr. Gershon was the CEO of the Daebrun Division who offered me the promotion to National Director of Student Finance as part of the agreement to settle my discrimination complaints.

He was a beefy man in his sixties with peach hued skin, pinkish cheeks, sea green eyes, and balding gray hair. In his previous career, he was a well-respected politician in the state of Texas who had a tough as nails approach to leadership and a reputation for shaking things up. As the CEO of Daebrun, he lived up to his reputation and many in our organization feared him.

A few minutes later, my desk phone rang. It was Dr. Gershon.

"Welcome back, Ebony," he said with a strong deep voice.

"Thank you, Dr. Gershon. It's good to be back."

"Why don't you make us a couple of coffees and come by my office. I take mine Black."

Make "us" a couple of coffees? I asked myself.

I couldn't believe that Dr. Gershon expected me to make him coffee like I was a glorified assistant, but I also didn't want to make any waves—especially during my first week reporting to him—so, after making the coffee, I went to Dr. Gershon's office, handed him his cup, and sat down in front of his desk.

"Mmm, that's good," he said, taking a sip. "Sorry I couldn't be here on your first day."

"It's okay, I had plenty of things to keep me busy. I'm looking forward to training and digging in."

"That's fine and dandy—love your ambition and there's gonna be plenty of time for that, but first things first—we need to introduce you to the rest of the executive team."

"Okay."

"I had IT give you access to my calendar. Schedule a one-hour meeting this afternoon with everyone under the Executive Leadership label."

"Sure, no problem."

Although I thought it was strange that Dr. Gershon gave me access to his calendar, I returned to my office and scheduled the meeting as instructed. Afterwards, I continued doing busy work until later that afternoon when I joined Dr. Gershon and the other bigwigs in the conference room where, surprise surprise, I was the only Black person in an executive leadership position.

Dr. Gershon kicked off the meeting with introductions.

"It's my pleasure to introduce you all to Ebony. As you know, she's the new National Director of Student Finance and she'll do just fine in this role so give her your support."

I thanked Dr. Gershon and smiled as various people sitting at the oval shaped table welcomed me. But there were others also sitting there who didn't say a word or even offer a friendly smile.

Dr. Gershon instructed everyone to introduce themselves and one by one each person stated their name, title, and for whatever reason, their academic credentials. And as I listened, I started to feel embarrassed.

46

Every single person on the executive leadership team had either a master's or doctorate degree and I had none, but not for a lack of trying. If you may recall, I tried several times to pursue my bachelor's at Daebrun, and each and every time, racism got in the way.

The last person to introduce himself was a muscle-bound man in his late twenties with an average height, mesmerizing green eyes, and a thick neck with broad shoulders. He had fair skin with a pink hue, freckles scattered across his nose and cheeks, and strawberry-blonde hair with a five o'clock shadow.

"It's great to finally put the face with the name," he said with a slight accent as he adjusted his red tie that appeared to be too tight. "I'm Travis Clayton, the National Director of HR. I have a Master of Science in HR Management and an MBA."

As soon as Travis introduced himself, I threw up in my mouth. Travis was the son-of-a-biscuit-eater who conspired with Dr. Taylor—the racist Chancellor at the Temple campus—and Michael—the spawn of Satan and my former employee—to fire me when I returned to work from mom's chemo appointment. But joke was on them, because I'm still here!

"It's nice to meet you, Travis." I lied through my teeth.

"Ebony, I can't remember, what is *your* Master's in?" He asked, putting me on the spot in front of everyone.

"I don't have one, not yet at least." I responded, trying to hide my embarrassment as I noticed multiple people slightly smirk. "But I plan to resume pursuing my bachelor's in finance soon."

The longer I sat at the table with the bigwigs, the more I realized how different I was from them, and I'm not talking about skin color. Each one of them had an air of superiority that painted them more as arrogant jerks than educated leaders. But even though I was the only one on the executive leadership team without a degree, I didn't let that discourage me because I knew that with the right training, I was capable of performing my job at an exceptional level even without a degree and nothing would stand in my way.

The executive leadership meeting got underway after the introductions were complete and Dr. Gershon instructed Travis to brief everyone on the urgent HR issue they discussed earlier that day.

Travis took a sip from his gallon-sized water bottle.

"The layoff has employees spooked," he said. "In the last two weeks, we've seen a record number of employees jumping ship and fake rumors are spreading that we're closing our doors."

The room erupted with yelling and frustration and as tempers flared, I noticed a few people giving me the side eye.

"Settle down," Dr. Gershon commanded. "Doesn't do us any good to kill the messenger. But if we don't restore employee confidence and quick, Corporate's going to be here breathing down our necks and nobody wants that."

Then, he turned to me.

"Ebony, I know the layoff is news to you, but you were once campus staff. How do you suggest we restore confidence?"

All eyes were on me once again, and I instantly felt nervous.

"Well, before I can weigh in," I replied. "Can you tell me why we had a layoff?"

Travis, who seemed to be annoyed by my question, quickly jumped in.

"Sure, Ebony. We had a significant number of unexpected expenditures in third quarter, making it necessary to reduce expenses."

The sharpness of his tone coupled with the side eyes I was still getting from others made me feel like the "unexpected expenditures" he was referring to had something to do with me and my settlement money.

But after asking a few more questions about the layoff to get clarity, I shared my thoughts. "I suppose that if I was still a campus employee, I would want some kind of assurance from you, Dr. Gershon, that more layoffs weren't expected to occur."

"I like it," Dr. Gershon replied. "Ebony, schedule an all-hands meeting for Monday morning—10 a.m.

Work with Cody on logistics, he knows what I need. I'll email you the information to prepare a PowerPoint this afternoon. Got it?"

"Yes," I acknowledged.

"Oh, and make arrangements for a continental style breakfast during the meeting at all campuses."

I sighed. His request was demeaning, and I knew everyone was waiting for a negative reaction from me.

"Yes, sir."

The meeting adjourned and as everyone returned to their respective offices, I returned to my office and sat down at my desk in a complete state of shock. I couldn't believe that I, the National Director of Student Finance, earning a whopping salary of eighty-six thousand a year, had unwittingly become Dr. Gershon's glorified Secretary and to make matters worse, I was being forced to work with Cody, the glorified grunt!

After scheduling the all-hands meeting as instructed, I documented everything that had occurred with Dr. Gershon in my Daily Log and then sent him the following email and saved it as proof that I was being required to make him coffee and perform secretarial duties because—as you know—the 'e' in email stands for evidence.

Dr. Gershon,

Just a quick note to give you an update. The access IT gave me to your calendar is working fine and I successfully scheduled the all-hands meeting, per your request, and made the catering arrangements. The only thing pending is the presentation you said you want me to prepare, so once I receive your draft I'll get it done.

Also, let me know if the coffee I'm making for you is too strong. I can add less coffee grounds, if needed.

Then, I dialed Cody's extension. I secretly hoped that he wouldn't answer, though, because I was already stressed out and didn't want to deal with anymore drama.

"IT department, Cody speaking," he answered in a professional voice, which ticked me off because I knew that *he* knew that I knew that *he* knew it was me calling since all the phones at Daebrun have caller ID.

"Hi Cody, it's Ebony. Dr. Gershon scheduled an all-hands meeting for Monday morning. He wants me to work with you on logistics. Did you see the invite?"

"Yeah." He said curtly.

"Okay, well just let me know when you have some time."

"I have time now. Meet me in the auditorium."

The auditorium, located in Building 1, had stadium seating and could easily accommodate over two hundred people. And although I wasn't thrilled with the idea of meeting with Cody, I was happy to escape the pompous posturing that was all around me in Building 2.

I arrived at the auditorium ten minutes later and saw Cody sitting in the last row at the top. So, I walked over to him.

"Hi Cody, thanks for meeting me."

"No worries. Follow me."

I followed Cody to the Control Room in the back of the auditorium. The Control Room was a booth where Cody and his team operated the auditorium's technical equipment including lights, speaker systems, computers, and projectors during events in a behind the scenes way.

Cody unlocked the door and invited me to have a seat in one of the chairs at the control panel. Then, he sat down in the chair next to me.

"Is there anything unusual Dr. G wants?" He asked.

50

"Define unusual, please."

"Okay. Let me explain what we typically do. My team will make sure lighting is good, internet speed is strong, and microphones are live. If he needs computer access for presentation purposes, we'll make sure the computer and projector are working properly, too. And if he wants video conferencing for the other campuses to attend or wants the event recorded, we'll need that information."

"Thanks for clarifying. He's planning to give a presentation, but the PowerPoint will not be ready until later this afternoon. I'll email it to you as soon as it's done. He also wants video conferencing."

"Got it. Anything else, Ebony?"

"No, that's it. Thank you."

I got up from my chair and began to walk out. Suddenly, Cody called out to me.

"Ebony, wait."

I turned around to face him.

"Yes?"

"I just wanted to say…I'm sorry," he said, looking at me with sorrowful eyes. "I just wish I knew what I was apologizing for. I mean, you hurt me, Ebony, and we just met so there's no way I did anything to deserve that."

"Didn't you?"

"Didn't I what? All I've done since the day you arrived is be nice to you and try to get to know you."

"I'm leaving now Cody."

He sighed.

"Okay, I won't bother you again, but I like you and I thought you liked me."

I was about to turn around and leave but then I noticed that he had another hard-on. Ugh!!

"Look man," I blurted out. "You and your fake hard-on need to go somewhere!"

Cody started to head for the door.

"I said I won't—Wait…What?"

He stopped in his tracks as his ears turned red.

"You heard me. That balled up sock in your pants isn't fooling anybody."

Cody's cheeks became flushed.

"Wow can't say I've heard that before. Give me a minute."

He looked around the room aimlessly for a few seconds before looking me dead in the eye.

"Are you seriously accusing me of having a *fake* hard-on?"

"Yes," I replied, raising my eyebrows, and giving him plenty of attitude.

"Is *that* what has you so pissed? Wow."

He took a deep breath and let it out quickly.

"Okay, listen Ebony. I don't have a sock in my pants and I'm not faking a fuckin' hard-on. I'm sorry I keep getting a boner in front of you. It's embarrassing, okay, but I'm not doing it on purpose. It's just that…well—you're hot."

I rolled my eyes.

"Yeah, right."

"Want me to prove it?"

I knew he was lying through his perfect teeth and since I was seriously thinking about quitting my job, I called his bluff.

"Yes, prove it."

"Are you sure?"

"Yes! Prove it!"

Cody walked over to the door and closed and locked it. Then, he walked over to the window overlooking the auditorium and closed the blinds as I watched.

"Come here," he said, leaning against the wall next to the window and slowly unzipping his jeans.

I quietly walked over as he reached out his hand to me. And when he gripped my hand and slid it into the opening in his jeans, I felt the width and length of his glorious shaft. It was not only large, but was also hard as a rock, hot as liquid fire, and throbbing against the palm of my hand. My breathing quickened, and I found myself in a heightened state of arousal.

I slowly pulled my hand out of his jeans intending to back away, but he gripped it and pulled me close.

"I want you, Ebony," he whispered, looking deep into my eyes before leaning in and passionately kissing me in a way that made me weak and caused my senses to soar.

With his hand still gripping mine, Cody pulled me to the floor and slowly peeled away my clothes as I closed my eyes, trembling with passion...and also fear. It was the first time since I left the safehouse that a man would see my body which was heavily scarred and bruised from years of domestic abuse.

As he continued peeling away my clothes and kissing my bare shoulders, I lowered my head as the voice inside my head got louder. *When he sees what you look like under all these clothes, he won't want you. Nobody wants you...*

Cody must've known something was wrong because he used his finger to gently lift up my chin.

"Open your eyes, Ebony," he softly said, cutting through the noise inside my head. "Look at me."

And when I did, I was set on fire as his smoldering blue eyes locked onto mine and he savored every inch of my body.

"You're the most beautiful woman I've ever seen," he whispered, caressing my curves with his hands and exploring my body with his mouth, kissing lower…and lower…and *lower*, until he reached my flower and my mind shut down.

Not once, in any of the relationships I'd been in, had a man ever told me that I was beautiful. Not even my ex-husband. And so I melted, pure putty in his hands as he molded me to his body like no one had ever done before.

Suddenly, the Control Room disappeared into a purplish pink haze and there was nothing…*no one*…but Cody and me, melding together in a chocolate and vanilla swirl, with all of the pleasure and none of the guilt, until our bodies exploded in pure ecstasy.

As I walked back my office in Building 2, feeling a lot less stressed and a lot more confident, I was ready to address the concerns I had with Dr. Gershon about the secretarial duties he was requiring me to perform, and I *knew* that once I made my case, he would understand where I was coming from…or so I thought.

CHAPTER 6

A NEW OPPORTUNITY

AFTER I RETURNED TO MY OFFICE, I MADE THE catering arrangements for the all-hands meeting and preparing the PowerPoint presentation as Dr. Gershon requested, I poked my head into Dr. Gershon's office.

"Do you have a minute?"

"Sure. Grab me some coffee and come on in."

"Okay."

After going to the breakroom and making a fresh pot of coffee, I returned to Dr. Gershon's office, walked in, and closed the door behind me. I handed him his cup and sat down in the chair in front of his desk.

"A closed-door conversation," he said after taking a sip of coffee. "Must be serious. What's on your mind?"

"I was hoping to get some clarification on my job."

"Okay, I'm all ears."

"Thank you. I haven't received my job description yet, but I was wondering when training for my national director duties would start."

"Training?" He asked, looking at me like I had just farted.

"Why, Ebony, you do realize that for Student Finance *you* are the trainer. So, are you proposing to train yourself?"

"No. I just thought someone from Corporate—"

"Well then," he said, cutting me off and smiling from ear to ear. "I'm glad that's settled. Anything else on your mind?"

Part of me wanted to punch him in his face. But the other part of me, the more logical part, overruled.

"Just one more thing. If you can email my job description to me, that would be great."

"Consider it done. I'll have Travis email it to you today."

Ten minutes later, I received Travis' email, and you know what I did with it, right? I saved it as tangible evidence.

The next two months were full of hope and promise both personally and romantically. At home, mom's health was holding steady both physically and mentally, and I thanked God every day for keeping her alive beyond the one-to-two-month life expectancy predicted by her doctor three months ago.

And romantically, things were great. Mom and Aiyden liked Cody a lot, even though Gabrielle still didn't trust him, and I was head over heels in love. And even though we rarely spent time together after work because I was spending precious time with mom, and kept our relationship under wraps at work because of Daebrun's No Fraternization Policy, we still found time every day to return to our love den, also known as the Control Room, to spend a few stolen moments of passionate time together.

Around the same time that I fell in love with Cody, I fell completely out of love with my job as National Director of Student Finance, even though I was performing it well despite the lack of training. You see, Dr. Gershon continued requiring me to make him coffee and manage his calendar. But he also added more secretarial duties to my plate, including planning his events, making his travel arrangements, and submitting his expense reports to Corporate every month. And when I tried to address the issue with him, things did not go well.

He accused me of not being a team player and told me to review my

56

job description paying particularly close attention to the last line that said I was responsible for performing "all other duties as assigned." And of course, I documented everything in my Daily Log and sent him emails to create the evidence I needed. But make no mistake about it, I hated reporting to Dr. Gershon with every fiber of my being and was actively looking for a way out.

But to be honest, reporting to Dr. Gershon wasn't the only reason I disliked my job. After five years of hell working in Student Finance, I was burned out and prayed for the chance to pursue a different career that not only paid well but allowed me to continue working at the Austin campus reporting to someone else besides Dr. Gershon.

The following week was Thanksgiving, and though it should have been a time for celebration and gathering, I was worried. Gabrielle and I cooked a wonderful Thanksgiving dinner for our family, but I noticed that Mom wasn't eating very much, and it concerned me. And I wished Cody was with me to give me a shoulder to lean on, and it sucked we couldn't spend our first holiday as a couple together as he had a second job and was scheduled to work that day.

When I returned to work from the holiday weekend on November 27, 2017, I received an email from Travis. The email was an internal job posting for a Regional Director of Quality Assurance and Compliance opening and was sent to all staff and faculty in the Daebrun division.

When I reviewed the details of the job opening and discovered that the position was housed at the Austin campus, had oversight of the Central Texas region—consisting of the Austin and Temple campuses— and reported to Corporate and not Dr. Gershon, it seemed like the answer to my prayers.

And when I read the job description and discovered that I met most of the qualifications in terms of professional experience and number of years in a leadership position, and that a bachelor's degree was preferred *but not required*, I emailed the job posting to Dr. Gershon and requested his permission to apply.

> *Good morning Dr. Gershon,*
>
> *I read the description for this internal job opening and believe that my skills and the requirements are a good match. May I proceed with applying?*
>
> *Thanks for your consideration.*
>
> *Sincerely,*
>
> *Ebony Ardoin, National Director of Student Finance*

Now, I bet your wondering why it was necessary for me to obtain Dr. Gershon's approval to apply, right? The answer is simple. Corporate changed their internal recruitment policy in February 2017, after the promotion they originally offered me to national director blew up in their faces thanks to Dr. Taylor. And after the promotion was yanked from me, Corporate updated their policy, requiring all employees to obtain their supervisor's approval before applying for any Corporate positions.

Fifteen minutes later, I received a one-sentence response to my email from Dr. Gershon.

> *Yes, you have my approval to apply.*

When I read Dr. Gershon's email and discovered that he approved my request, I was shocked. You see, Dr. Gershon loved the job I was doing as the National Director of Student Finance almost as much as he loved having me as his Black workhorse. So, I'm guessing that the reason he approved my request to apply was because he believed the chances of Corporate selecting me for the position were low.

After all, the regional position was responsible for ensuring that *all departments* at the Austin and Temple campuses were operating in compliance with federal, state, and regulatory requirements and my experience in management was limited to student finance. But regardless of the reason Dr. Gershon approved my request, you know me—I wasn't going to look a gift horse in the mouth. So, I happily replied to the email from Travis Clayton and officially applied for the position.

Good morning Travis,

I am interested in applying for the Regional Director of Quality Assurance and Compliance position. I've been seeking an opportunity to change career fields and believe that my skills and the position requirements are a great match. Attached is the email from Dr. Gershon approving my candidacy and my resume for your review.

As you consider this management placement, please note the accomplishments outlined in my most recent performance review which is also attached.

A career with emphasis in student finance operations and with exposure to various higher education environments has sharpened my leadership skills. If you are seeking a regional director who is top in her field, understands regulatory requirements and technology, and is as career-committed as it takes to achieve overall success, please consider what I bring to the table.

Respectfully yours,
Ebony Ardoin, National Director of Student Finance

Then, I saved my email as evidence that I applied for the position and documented everything in my Daily Log.

Two days later, I received a call from Frank Adams, the Corporate Vice President of Quality Assurance, acknowledging receipt of my resume and scheduling an over-the-phone interview with him for the next day.

The interview with Frank went extremely well. Not only was he impressed with my qualifications and achievements, but he also seemed to take an instant liking to me, especially my voice.

"If you don't mind me saying," he said. "You have a voice that belongs in radio."

"I'll take that as a compliment. Thank you!"

"It is a compliment. You know, you can learn a lot about a person from their voice."

"Really? What does my voice tell you about me?"

He paused for a minute.

"Your voice says you're a tall blonde workaholic," he answered.

I giggled.

"Well, I'm not *that* tall."

"Great interview, Ebony. I'll be in touch."

When Frank said he thought I was a tall blonde workaholic...basically, he thought I was White, part of me was stunned that my name didn't give him his first clue that I wasn't. And a part of me wanted to tell him that his assumption couldn't have been any further from the truth.

But the other part of me, the more logical part, overruled.

The next day, I received an email from Frank instructing me to complete a Competitive Intelligence (CI) Assessment. I had never done a CI Assessment before and had no idea what the heck it was, but I completed it anyway and gave it my best shot. I must've done well on the assessment because a week later, I received another email from Frank instructing me to complete a CI Profile and although I had no clue what that was either, I completed it, nonetheless.

A week later, I received another email from Frank that made me jump for joy as I realized my candidacy for the regional director position was seriously being considered by Corporate.

> *Ebony,*
>
> *I'm pleased to inform you that you are a finalist for the RDQAC position. Final interviews will be conducted in person at Corporate. Brea Martin, our Corporate Talent Recruiter, will be in touch to secure your travel arrangements.*
>
> *Thank you for your interest in working for Corporate.*
>
> *Frank Adams*
> *Corporate Vice President of Quality Assurance*

When I received Frank's email, I was beyond thrilled. And after saving a copy as proof that I was a finalist and documenting it in my Daily Log, I forwarded it to Dr. Gershon as an FYI. A couple of hours later, I received the following response:

> *Ebony,*
>
> *Congratulations! You should be proud. If it doesn't work out, we're happy to have you continue leading student finance.*

Dr. Gershon was being a Debbie Downer in his email, and it was clear that he thought things wouldn't work out. But I had faith in God and wasn't going to let Negative Nancy kill my joy, so I immediately called Mom to share the good news.

"Mom! You'll never guess in a million years what happened!"

"You win the lotto, child?"

"No, something better! I'm a finalist for the regional director position! I've got a real shot at this!"

"I'm so proud of ya', honey. God is good! How much does it pay?"

"I don't know. We haven't discussed salary yet. There is a problem, though. The final interviews are in Florida, and I don't want to leave you."

"Ebony, I want ya' to go. I'm feelin' fine these days and ya' know Gabby's gonna take great care of us."

"But mom, what if something happens and—"

"Listen to me. You can't live your life worrying all the time. When ya' worry, you're tellin' God you don't trust Him. Do you trust God?"

"Yes."

"So trust that whatever is supposed to happen will happen whether you're here or in Florida. Okay?"

"Okay, mom."

For the first time in a long time, everything was right in the world. I still had a life with Mom in it, I finally had love with a man I adored, and I was on the verge of having an exciting and new career reporting to Corporate. Yes, everything was definitely right in the world, and my future was looking very bright...or so I thought.

CHAPTER 7

THE BEGINNING OF THE END

ON DECEMBER 10, 2017, I FLEW TO TAMPA TO COMPLETE the final round of in-person interviews for the Regional Director of Quality Assurance & Compliance position. According to my itinerary, Frank Adams, the Corporate VP of Quality Assurance, was going to pick me up in the hotel lobby at 8 a.m. and take me to breakfast to conduct a second, more detailed interview to discuss my qualifications. After breakfast, we would go to Corporate where I would have an in-depth interview with the Chief Compliance Officer.

Two and a half hours later, my plane landed, and I took an Uber to the hotel. And when I walked into the lobby to check in, I was feeling the Christmas spirit as I admired the beautiful holiday decorations and lights.

A short time later, I settled into my room and ordered dinner from room service before calling Gabrielle to check on Mom and Aiyden.

"How's everything going, sis?"

"Mom's doin' fine. She's sleepin' a little more than usual, but the hospice nurse said that's normal. Aiyden's great. He just finished eating and is doin' his homework."

"Okay great, kiss Mom and little man for me. Love you."

"Love you, too."

After hanging up, I started flipping through the channels trying to find something interesting to watch while I waited for my dinner to arrive. Suddenly, my cell phone rang. It was Cody.

"Hey Babe, you have a good flight?"

"I did, thank you for asking."

"Well, you know me, I'm easy for you. I miss you, Babe."

"I miss you, too. Sounds like you're driving. Where ya' going?"

"To get some gas. Thought I'd check on you while I was out."

"You're so sweet, Cody. I can't wait to be back in your arms."

"I can't wait to be back *in* you."

"Oh-h-h, that sounds amazing. I'm looking forward to it."

"Good luck on your interview. You got this. Bye, Babe."

Shortly after hanging up with Cody, my dinner arrived. I was starving and wolfed down the mushroom Swiss burger and fries like I hadn't eaten in weeks. Then, I started watching TV.

Suddenly, my cell phone rang again. It was Latoya Johnson, my old coworker. When I met her four years ago, she was in her twenties and pregnant with an average height, mahogany skin she slathered with cocoa butter, and hypnotic gray eyes she said came from her mother. She also had chestnut brown hair that flowed down her back, a larger-than-life personality, and a reputation for being ghetto fabulous.

Latoya and I were the only Black people working in the Student Finance Office at the Austin campus back then, and we were both victims of racial discrimination. But we fought back using the same attorney and after Daebrun settled with each of us a month ago, she resigned from her position at Daebrun and dropped off the face of the earth, ghosting me. So, when I saw Latoya's name on the caller ID, I was fit to be tied.

"Toy, where the hell have you been? I've been leaving all kinds of messages for you! Had me worried sick!"

"Gurrl, I went into hiding just in case those devils changed their mind about my money. I'm happy now, though. That forty-thousand-dollar check cleared the bank and we just got back from one hell of a vacation. I'm sorry I made ya' crazy ass worry."

"It's okay, I understand. I'm glad you had a great time. So, Daebrun settled with you for forty thousand?"

"Whoops, I wasn't supposed to say nothin' was I? Gurrl, keep that shit on the down low, okay?"

"You know I will."

"Well since you know mine, how much did you get?"

I didn't have the heart to tell Latoya that she settled for an amount that was way too low and that I got two hundred thousand. But I'm guessing Daebrun lowballed her because they knew she was desperate for money and would probably accept the first offer they made without negotiating. So, I lied.

"I got the same amount as you, Toy."

"That's good to hear. Did I tell you I got a new job? I'm a leasing agent at an apartment complex. I start next week."

"Congratulations, Toy! That's great news!"

"Yeah it is—but anyway, how's ya' momma doin'?"

"She's hanging in there. We just got back from an incredible vacation, ourselves. We went back home to Shreveport, and she was thrilled. We're taking it one day at a time but she's doing great."

"I'm so glad to hear that. I know ya' momma's real special. How's work goin'?"

"Thanks, Toy. I appreciate that. Work is great, too. You're not going to believe this, but guess who has a man? This girl right here!"

"Gurrl, look at you! Got money AND a man! Anybody I know?"

"Do you know Cody, the Director of IT?"

"Sure, I do! Great guy! Got a beautiful wife, too. He introduce you to one of his techie friends?"

My stomach sank. "You must be thinking of someone else, Toy. Cody's not married."

"If he's that fine ass White guy that looks like the man in that *Rocky* movie, Dolph—Dolph somethin' or another, he's married. I met his wife at the Christmas party last year."

"Well, he's definitely not married now 'cause he's dating *me*. Maybe he was married then, but he's definitely not now."

"Gurrl, you datin' a White man? Go on with ya' bad self! If you like it, I love it! I'm happy for ya'."

"Thanks, Toy. Talk to you later."

After hanging up, my stomach was in a ball of nerves as Latoya's words rang loudly in my head.

If he's that fine ass White guy that looks like the man in that Rocky movie Dolph—Dolph somethin' or another, he's married.

I took a hot shower to relax my body and my mind, set the alarm on my phone to wake me up at 6 a.m., and climbed into bed, determined to get a good night sleep before my interviews in the morning. But as I laid in bed, I found myself unable to sleep, as so many thoughts crowded my mind.

He never invites me over to his place—he said he has roommates.

We rarely go on dates at night—he said he has a second job.

He never answers my calls at night—they go straight to voicemail.

He only calls me at night when he's driving to or from somewhere.

He has two phones—he said one is his work phone.

He never introduces me to anyone.

As concerns about Cody continued to mount, I sat up in the bed, grabbed my cell phone from the nightstand, and tried to call him, but as usual the call went straight to voicemail.

I tried again—the same thing happened. After trying a third time, I left a voice message. "Cody, call me as soon as you get this message. It's urgent."

Afterwards, I grabbed a couple of melatonin gummies from my purse to help me fall asleep, laid my head back down on the pillow, and closed my eyes, tears streaming down my face.

"Please let Toy be wrong," I prayed to God with passion and a heart that was breaking. "Please don't let Cody be married. In Jesus holy, mighty, and beautiful name I pray, Amen." Fifteen minutes later, the melatonin kicked in and I finally fell asleep.

The next morning, my alarm went off at 6 a.m. sharp and I jumped up and started getting dressed. I had just put toothpaste on my toothbrush when my cell phone rang. It was Cody. I put down my toothbrush and answered the phone without saying a word.

"Babe? Are you there? Can you hear me?"

"Yes, I hear you."

"I just got your message. Everything okay?"

"I—I don't know." I swallowed hard. "I—I need to ask you something and I need the honest truth."

"You can ask me anything, Babe."

I took a deep breath and let it out.

"Cody, are you married?"

The phone went dead for several minutes, and I thought he had hung up on me.

"Let's talk when you get home. I'll explain everything, I promise."

"No Cody!" I yelled as tears flooded my cheeks. "Explain everything now, I deserve that much! Are you married?"

Cody paused for a moment.

"Yes. I'm so sorry, Babe, I was going to tell you—"

I quickly hung up the phone.

And as I stood in front of the bathroom mirror above the sink, barely able to see myself through my tears, I cried like there was no tomorrow.

Fifteen minutes later, I realized it was almost 7 a.m. and I still needed to get dressed for my interviews, because no matter what was happening with Cody, I wanted the regional director job and wasn't going to let him ruin my chances. So, after grabbing some ice from the ice machine down the hall, I held the ice under my eyes for several minutes to reduce puffiness, put some allergy eye drops in my eyes to reduce redness, and finished getting dressed.

I made it to the lobby at 7:50 a.m. and sat near the door as I waited for Frank Adams, the Corporate VP of Quality Assurance who said I sounded like a tall blonde workaholic, to arrive. Despite everything that had happened with Cody, I was actually very hungry and was looking forward to breakfast with Frank.

As I waited for Frank to arrive, I received about twenty text messages from Cody begging me to forgive him, saying how sorry he was for lying, telling me he never meant to hurt me, yadda yadda yadda. And in between scrolling through his messages, I continued to watch people exiting and entering the hotel.

A few minutes later, a heavyset man in his mid-fifties wearing a black power suit with a silk plum tie walked through the door holding a cell phone in his hand. He was about five foot nine with gray hair and a receding hairline. I had a feeling he was Frank Adams so when he walked by without giving me a second thought, I called out to him.

"Frank?"

He turned around, and when he saw me, his eyes widened.

"Ebony?" He asked, almost in disbelief.

"Yes."

I gave him my best fake smile as I walked over and offered him my hand to shake.

"It's great to finally meet you."

He flinched, grabbing my hand for just a split second, like he was afraid to touch me.

68

"It's good to meet you, Ebony."

There was an awkward silence for at least thirty seconds, so I tried to break the ice.

"I'm looking forward to breakfast. Where are we going?"

"Oh, sorry, there's been a change in plans. I have a scheduling conflict so unfortunately, we won't be going to breakfast, but we have vending machines at Corporate. I'm sure you can find something to your liking there."

"Okay, what about my second interview with you?"

"I'm pretty sure I have enough information. A second interview was just protocol but it's really not necessary."

We exited the hotel lobby and as we walked to this car, there was no doubt in my mind—he was disappointed that I was Black. I mean, when he grabbed my hand to shake it, he let it go so fast like my brown skin might rub off on him if he held on too long.

The drive to Corporate was just as uncomfortable as I thought it would be. Frank barely said two words to me, and I didn't try to make small talk. After all, what was the point? I was sitting next to a racist and there wasn't anything I could do or say to make the situation better. So, I used my phone to type an email to myself, documenting everything that happened with Frank starting from the time he arrived at the hotel. Then I emailed it to my personal email so that I wouldn't forget any details and could copy and paste it into my Daily Log when I got home.

Twenty excruciatingly long minutes later, we arrived at a five-story brick and glass building located downtown in the urban core of Tampa. And after following Frank into the building and taking the elevator to the third floor, he pawned me off on his administrative assistant, a White woman in her mid-twenties with long brown hair, who was not only surprised that she was now responsible for escorting me to my interview but was also very kind offering me a pastry and a cup of coffee in the breakroom after I explained that I was starving.

For the next hour, I sat in the breakroom at Corporate by myself, staring out the window and trying to hold back the tears as I thought about Cody's betrayal, lies, and deceit. And to be honest, part of me wanted to be vindictive and contact his wife to tell her about his treachery to destroy his marriage.

Cody didn't know, but after we gave in to passion the first time in the Control Room that day, I looked him up in our student database when I returned to my office, hoping that he had pursued his bachelor's degree in IT at Daebrun like I was trying to do. And sure enough, I found him *and* his personal information, including his full legal name, social security number, date of birth, *and physical address*.

But the other part of me, the part that was still very much in love with him, overruled. Although I couldn't bear the thought of being a homewrecker, I was hoping there was some logical explanation I could live with—and that somehow, some way, Cody and I would make it through the storm.

At 9:45 a.m., Frank's administrative assistant returned to the breakroom and escorted me to the office of Rick Kashinsky, the Chief Compliance Officer, for my interview. Rick was the man who came to the Temple campus and informed me that I was being investigated for allegations of misconduct and unethical behavior after I emailed my discrimination complaint to the CEO at Corporate. Rick was a tall well-groomed man with olive skin, short brown hair, green eyes, and a commanding presence. He wore a gray tailored suit with a burgundy tie and reminded me of a secret service agent because of the earpiece in one of his ears.

When Rick saw me and the administrative assistant standing in his doorway, he invited me in.

"Ebony, it's good to see you. Have a seat."

"Thank you."

I walked in and sat down in front of his desk.

"So let me tell you about the position," he said, diving right in.

"The Regional Director of Quality Assurance and Compliance is the first of several regional director positions we plan to create over time as we grow.

70

It is a Corporate-level position that has oversight of the Central Texas region and is responsible for ensuring that all departments are operating in compliance with federal, state, and regulatory requirements. Because of its importance, the person selected to fill the position will report to me. However, the salary and associated expenses, including mileage, will be determined and paid by the Daebrun division. Understand?"

"Yes, it makes sense."

"Do you have any questions?"

"Yes, just one. What is the expected date to fill the position?"

"January first."

Rick leaned back in his chair.

"I must say I was rather surprised when your resume came across my desk, Ebony. You having any more issues I should be aware of?"

When Rick asked me this pointed question, I knew he was *really* asking if I had experienced anymore racism at Daebrun, and part of me really wanted to cry out, yes!

But I didn't, because I didn't have enough evidence to prove anything racist had happened. So, I put on my best fake smile and lied.

"No, things are great in student finance. I'm just looking for an opportunity to grow as a leader and expand my knowledge of other departments."

Rick seemed satisfied with my response and proceeded to ask me numerous questions about my leadership style and management skills. He must've been satisfied with my answers to those questions, too, because the interview was still going strong an hour later, and he had lunch brought in for us to continue talking as he reviewed the sample statistical charts and graphs I created when I worked at the Temple campus to measure employee performance.

"This is the type of data we need to see in all departments," Rick commented as he flipped through the pages of my portfolio. "I'm thoroughly impressed."

When the interview ended two and a half hours later, he told me that

Frank Adams, the Corporate VP of Quality Assurance, would contact me to discuss next steps. Then, he called Frank to his office to collect me and take me back to my hotel.

Frank and I left Rick's office and entered the elevator. "How did your interview go?" He asked, giving me the side eye.

"I think it went very well."

"Well, if things don't work out, you can always stay in student finance."

His comment was nearly identical to what Dr. Gershon had said in his email to me after I informed him that I was a finalist for the regional position, and instantly put my radar on high alert.

The drive back to the hotel was quiet. Neither one of us said a word the entire time. And when we made it back to the hotel, I opened my door before the car came to a full stop and put a whole lot of 'racist be gone' between me and that jerk.

Even though I was scheduled to stay in the hotel one more night, I was ready to get the hell out of Tampa. So, I checked out early, took an Uber to the airport, and paid to change my airline ticket to the next available flight. And even though things with Cody seemed grim, I still had hope that things could work out. After all, it's always darkest just before dawn...or so I thought.

CHAPTER 8

THE END OF LOVE

MY PLANE LANDED IN AUSTIN AT 7:30 P.M. AND WHEN I made it home from the airport, Aiyden ran up the steps from the family room and threw himself into my open arms.

"Mommy!" He yelled, giving me a much-needed hug in the small entryway. "I don't want to play with your phone!"

"You don't?"

"No! I got my own phone, see?" He lifted his phone up with pride to show me.

"Oh yeah!" I said, pretending I didn't remember. "I guess I forgot."

Aiyden laughed as he jumped down the steps and continued watching TV and I walked up the steps into the living room where Gabrielle was laying on the couch watching *Madea's Family Reunion*.

Gabrielle took one look at me and knew something was wrong.

"Eb, you okay?" She asked, sitting up on the couch.

"I'll tell you in a minute," I replied, choking back the tears. "Let me go check on Mom first."

I walked into my bedroom and saw Mom sleeping peacefully on the bed. I was grateful to God that she was asleep because Mom knew me better than anyone else and I didn't want to cause her to worry.

After kissing Mom on the forehead, I returned to the living room and sat down next to Gabrielle.

"He's married, Gabby," I softly said, as tear after tear rolled down my cheeks. "Cody's married."

Gabrielle grabbed my hand.

"Are ya' sure?"

I began to sob.

"Yes, I'm sure. He admitted it."

"Damn. I knew my instincts were right. I never trusted his ass!"

"Please don't say I told you so."

"I won't, but if it were me, I'd tell his wife. I'd hire a private eye to find out where he lives and show up on his doorstep."

"I already know his address."

"Great! Give it to me, I'll tell his wife myself."

"Thanks, Gabby, but no. I don't want to do that."

"Why, Eb? Do you still want him?"

I paused for a moment.

"I don't know. Maybe there's some reasonable answer that I haven't considered yet. Maybe they're separated or something."

Gabrielle gave me a hug as I continued sobbing.

"Don't worry about it tonight, sis. Go rest, it'll keep 'til the mornin'. And don't worry about Aiyden. I got him."

I walked into my room and glanced at mom, still sound asleep on the bed before going into the master bathroom, closing the door, and turning on the hot water in the shower to wash the day away. And as steam rose as I slowly got undressed, the eucalyptus oil in the shower turned my bathroom into my very own spa and helped me relax.

That is—until I heard Mom yelling at the top of her lungs at someone who wasn't Gabrielle or Aiyden.

"Get outta here!" Mom screamed. "I don't know you!"

I grabbed my robe from the door and tried to throw it on as I ran out of the bathroom half naked and Gabrielle ran in.

"Mom?" Gabrielle asked, looking alarmed.

"Don't worry, Gabby. They're gone," Mom replied, breathing hard. "I chased 'em away."

"Chased who away, mom? I asked.

"Those thieves," she replied, tearing up. "Are they stealing your stuff, too?"

"I'm callin' the doctor." Gabrielle said, before leaving the room to get her phone.

I didn't know what was happening inside mom's head, all I knew was that she was distraught, and I wanted to comfort her. So, I sat on the bed and gently hugged her.

"Everything's alright," I said before giving her a kiss on the cheek. "You protected us, mom, no one's here now. You chased them away."

Mom smiled.

I stayed in the room with Mom until Gabrielle returned and informed us that the hospice nurse was on her way. Then, I returned to the bathroom and turned off the now lukewarm water running in the shower.

Thirty minutes later, the hospice nurse arrived, took mom's vitals, and gave her an additional dose of morphine to make her comfortable and manage her pain. Afterwards, we went into the living room to talk, and the hospice nurse gently explained that hallucinations were an indicator that Mom was progressing in the end-of-life process. She said if they got worse and Mom became overly agitated or upset, she could prescribe medication to sedate her.

After the hospice nurse left, my anxiety was through the roof, and I was shaking like a leaf. So, after kissing Aiyden goodnight and thanking

Gabrielle for tucking him into bed, I took the hot shower I originally planned to take and did everything I could to calm my nerves. I inhaled eucalyptus vapors. I did deep breathing exercises. I listened to soothing music. But in the end, nothing worked. My world was crumbling around me and there was no one to pick up the broken pieces and put it back together.

After my shower, I put on my pajamas, climbed into bed with mom, and laid my head on her shoulder as my heart raced and tears flow from my eyes. And even though she was sound asleep as I wrap my arm around her, I was comforted by her presence.

The next day, I went to work, even though it was the last place I wanted to be and sent an email to Frank Adams, the Corporate VP of Quality Assurance, and Rick Kashinsky, the Chief Compliance Officer at Corporate, thanking them for their hospitality during the interview process.

Good morning Frank and Rick,

Thank you for your hospitality during my visit to Corporate yesterday. Meeting with each of you and learning about the various layers of quality assurance and compliance made for an exciting and informative day.

I look forward to hearing from you once a decision has been made regarding the Regional Director of Quality Assurance and Compliance position and thank you again for considering my candidacy.

Sincerely,
Ebony Ardoin, National Director of Student Finance

Five minutes after sending the email, my cell phone rang.

It was Cody.

"Babe, are you back from Florida?"

"Yes."

"Are you on campus?"

"Yes."

"Please meet me in the Control Room so we can talk."

I sighed.

"Okay, I'm on my way."

Ten minutes later, I arrived at the Control Room where Cody was waiting for me, looking exactly like I felt. I walked in without saying a word and sat down at the control panel. As he sat down in the chair next to mine, the awkward silence between us was deafening.

He looked at me through watery eyes and attempted to grab my hand, but I gently pulled it away.

"Babe," he said as a tear fell down his cheek. "I'm so sorry I hurt you."

"Are you?" I said as my own tears began to fall. "Or are you just sorry you got caught?"

"I'm truly sorry, Ebony. I was selfish and I'm sorry."

"How long have you been married? Do you have kids? Is she Black?"

"I've been married for nine months. I don't have any kids. She's not Black, she's half Korean and half White."

"You started cheating on your wife nine months after you were married? Why would you do that? Do you even love her?"

He lowered his head, looking down at the ground.

"I do love her, but there's no passion, especially not the kind I get with you. I never planned to cheat but when I saw you, I couldn't resist. I don't want to lose you, Ebony. You're the most incredible lover I've ever had. Maybe we can continue to see each other."

I shook my head as I stood up.

"Absolutely not! So, thanks for lying to me, thanks for using me, thanks for hurting me. You know, Gabby thinks I should tell your wife."

"Oh God, please don't!" He cried out hysterically. "I'm sorry Ebony! Please don't ruin my marriage! My wife will never forgive me!"

When I saw Cody begging me not to tell his wife, the rose-colored glasses I was wearing came off and I saw him for what he was—a selfish man who wanted to have his cake and eat it, too. He wanted the security he had with his wife, but he also wanted the passion and fire he got from me. A former U.S. president whose name I refuse to mention once said that emotionally disturbed women make the best lovers. So, in a way I understood the reason Cody was addicted to me. With all the emotional baggage I'd carried since I was a girl, I realized I was this White man's catnip.

I walked out of the Control Room, leaving Cody behind, and I'm not going to lie…part of me wanted to embrace the darkness and show up on his doorstep like Gabrielle suggested to tell his wife about all the things we did and the various places on my body his mouth had been. But the other part of me, the part that Mom raised to understand that two wrongs don't make a right, overruled because I didn't want to hurt his wife, someone who didn't deserve the pain that telling her would cause.

When I returned to my office, I closed the door and then called Gabrielle as tears streamed down my cheeks.

"It's over Gabby. Cody and I are through."

"I'm so sorry, Eb."

"He didn't even try to fight for me. He just wanted a side piece of chocolate ass. Guess King Marcus was right."

"No, he wasn't, Eb. Cody's a jerk, but don't give up. Kissin' frogs until one turns into a prince is normal. Do you know how many frogs I've kissed? And not one of them has turned into a fuckin' prince. Why do you think I'm still single?"

I chuckled.

"Thanks for the reminder. That actually makes me feel better. Love you."

"Love ya', too, sis."

After talking to Gabrielle, I felt a lot better about my situation with Cody and with life in general, and decided not to spend any more time focusing on what was wrong in the world and instead chose to focus on what was right.

And the incredible interview I had with Rick Kashinsky for the Regional Director position was something that was right. So right, in fact, that I had hope that an offer of employment would be extended to me in a matter of days. Things were looking up, and I was finally going to get the hell away from Dr. Gershon…or so I thought.

CHAPTER 9

THE END OF HOPE

OVER THE NEXT WEEK AND A HALF, MOM CONTINUED to hallucinate on an off at home and Cody avoided me like I had the plague at work. But there were times when our paths crossed during meetings, and he couldn't avoid me. And when I noticed him wearing suits to work instead of the blue jeans he normally wore, it didn't take a rocket scientist to know that he was going on interviews during work hours.

So, on the Friday before Christmas when he stopped by my office and informed me that he had resigned from Daebrun, I wasn't the least bit surprised. I knew he wanted to put as much distance between us as possible in an effort to keep his wife from finding out about our short-lived affair. I'm just glad he had the decency to tell me himself before I found out through the grape vine—I deserved that much from him. I never told Mom or Aiyden about Cody's betrayal. I just hoped the memory of him would fade away with time.

Although I wasn't feeling the Christmas spirit, I put my feelings on the backburner and worked with Gabrielle to make Christmas as wonderful as possible for Aiyden and mom. Christmas was mom's favorite holiday and since we didn't know how many more Christmases she would have we did our very best to make it special.

On December 27, 2017, I returned to work from the holiday weekend and received a call from Frank Adams, the Corporate VP of Quality Assurance and racist jerk.

"I have good news and not-so-good news. Which do you want first?"

"I'll take the good news first."

"Rick Kashinsky is very interested in you for the regional position and is planning to make you an offer."

"That's wonderful news! Thank you!"

"Now for the bad news. There's gonna be one more interview. Dr. Gershon wants the new Chancellor at the Temple campus to meet you and be included in the interview process. I know you had some issues with the previous Chancellor at that campus and hope this won't be too uncomfortable for you. Rick agreed to Dr. Gershon's request."

"Okay."

"So, I just want to make sure you're still interested in the position."

"Yes, I'm still interested."

"Are you sure? Because working for Corporate's not easy. It requires a lot of work, and I don't want to see you get burned out."

"I'm no stranger to hard work, Frank. As the National Director of Student Finance, I'm responsible for all campuses—not just Austin and Temple."

"Yes, but as the regional director you'll be responsible for *all departments* and that's a lot more work."

"Thanks for your concern, Frank, but I'm up to the challenge."

It was obvious Frank was trying to dissuade me from pursuing the regional director position, probably because I was Black. But what on earth was Dr. Gershon doing?

Immediately after hanging up with Frank, I documented the conversation in my Daily Log and sent him the following email as proof that he said I was going to be offered the regional position.

Good morning Frank,

It was great speaking with you this morning! Thank you for informing me that Rick Kashinsky is going to make me an offer for the Regional Director of Quality Assurance and Compliance position. I am excited about this opportunity and am definitely interested.

Per our conversation, it is my understanding that one more interview is scheduled with the Chancellor of the Temple campus. I will let you know when the interview is complete.

Thanks for the great news!

Sincerely,

Ebony Ardoin, National Director of Student Finance

Later that afternoon, I received a phone call from the receptionist at the Temple campus, letting me know my interview was scheduled for the following week with Danielle Kent, the new Chancellor who replaced Dr. Taylor after she was fired.

Two days later, I drove to the Temple campus, an hour commute from Austin, for my interview with the new Chancellor, Danielle Kent, a thick woman in her mid-forties with a shorter than average height, ivory skin, green eyes, and bobbed brunette hair. The interview was a complete waste of time and gas.

Not only had she not reviewed my resume and had no idea what my background and qualifications were, but when I offered to give her one of the extra copies I had in my briefcase, she declined, saying that it wasn't necessary.

I did most of the talking trying to keep the interview afloat since she wasn't asking me any questions, but it was clear that she wasn't interested. It was by far the strangest interview I had ever attended.

After my interview, I left the Temple campus and grabbed a burger and fries from the drive-up window of a fast-food restaurant. I made it to my office at the Austin campus an hour later, documented the strange interview in my Daily Log, and sent the following email to Frank Adams as evidence.

Good morning Frank,

I completed my interview this morning with Danielle Kent, Chancellor of the Temple Campus, for the Regional Director of Quality Assurance & Compliance position, per your instructions.

I look forward to hearing from you regarding the offer of employment you discussed with me.

Sincerely,
Ebony Ardoin, National Director of Student Finance

I was just about to call Gabrielle to check on Mom when Amanda Ross, the Chancellor of the Austin campus, walked in. Amanda was a full-figured woman in her mid-forties with a rosy complexion, amber eyes as bright as the sun, and shoulder-length brown hair with a side bang. She had a pair of reading glasses sitting on top of her head, wore a red designer suit with black flat shoes, and had more diamonds on her fingers, ears, neck, and wrists than my jewelry collector friend had in stock.

"Hello Ebony."

"It's good to see you, Amanda. What brings you to this neck of the woods?"

"Just wanted to give you some good news. I spoke with Danielle, and we've agreed to a fifteen percent salary increase plus mileage reimbursement for the regional position.

The costs will be split between our campuses, but your paycheck will be issued from Austin."

"That's fantastic news, thank you for sharing!"

When Amanda said the regional position came with a fifteen percent salary increase, I was so excited I wanted to do a backflip! A fifteen percent salary increase meant that my new salary as the regional director would be ninety-eight thousand nine hundred dollars a year—just shy of six-figures!

Immediately after Amanda left my office, you know what I did, right? I sent her an email confirming our conversation as proof of the salary I was offered. Now, I bet your thinking that everything from this point forward regarding the regional position was a walk in the park, right? Wrong.

New Year's Day came and went and when I returned to work on January 2, 2018, I still had not received the offer of employment that Frank Adams, the Corporate VP of Quality Assurance, said I would receive back on December 27th. So, I sent the following email to him to follow up on the status:

Good morning Frank,

Just a quick note to follow up on the status of the employment offer you said I would be receiving during our telephone conversation on December 27th, 2017, regarding the Regional Director of Quality Assurance and Compliance position.

Please provide me with a status update. Thank you.

Sincerely,

Ebony Ardoin, National Director of Student Finance

Forty-five minutes later, I received the following response to my email from Frank Adams:

Ebony—

We can't move forward until we hear back from Danielle Kent. I've called and emailed her several times. I have not heard back as of yet.

I'll let you know as soon as she responds.

Frank

Two more weeks went by, and I still had not received the employment offer for the Regional Director of Quality Assurance and Compliance position or even so much as a status update from Frank Adams. At this point, red flags were popping up everywhere, as an all too familiar feeling set in. But there's no way I was experiencing racism again, right? I mean, everyone knows lightning never strikes the same place twice...or so I thought.

CHAPTER 10

THE END OF LIES

ON JANUARY 17, 2018, ALMOST THREE WEEKS AFTER I was told by Frank Adams, the Corporate VP of Quality Assurance, that I would be receiving an employment offer for the regional position, Amanda Ross, the Chancellor at the Austin campus, stopped by my office out of the blue. She looked troubled and when I noticed she wasn't wearing the eighteen-carat diamond ring she usually wore, I assumed it had something to do with the look on her face.

"Are you okay, Amanda?" I asked. "Did something happen to your ring?"

"No, it's being cleaned."

"I'm glad nothing happened. For a minute, I thought it was stolen."

She sat down in front of my desk and folded her hands in her lap.

"I do need to talk to you, Ebony."

"About what?"

"The regional position. There's been some changes I don't think you're going to like."

"What changes?"

"It's complicated. Danielle and I discussed it again and we—we just can't justify giving you a salary increase if you accept the position. Your current salary is already way above the budgeted amount."

"So, I'll be promoted without a salary increase?"

"Not exactly. If you accept the position, it won't be a promotion it'll be a demotion and your current salary will be reduced by fifteen percent. If you think about it, it makes sense. In your national position, you're responsible for *all campuses* in the Daebrun division and your salary is equally split between each cost center. In the regional position, you'll only be responsible for Austin and Temple, and we'll be liable for paying your salary, which as I mentioned, is already too high."

As Amanda talked, I weighed the pros and cons of accepting the regional position in my head and concluded that sometimes there's more important things to consider than money, like job satisfaction and reporting to a boss you actually like. And even though my income would be reduced by about thirteen thousand dollars a year, I would still be earning a decent salary.

"I know you're disappointed," Amanda continued. "Can I let Corporate know you're no longer interested in the position?"

"No," I replied. "I'm still interested. I'm not worried about the demotion or salary decrease. I'm more interested in professional development."

You should've seen the look on Amanda's face when I said I was still interested in the regional position. She looked like she had just seen a ghost! And that's when weirdness entered the scene.

"But—but Ebony, it—it—it's not professional development really. The scope has changed, too. If you accept, you'll be wasting your skills, doing things like…counting the number of erasers in each classroom and making sure we have the correct number of desks."

When Amanda said I'd be counting erasers and desks if I accepted the regional position, I began to suspect that there was something more sinister, more nefarious at play. And as she sat there, insulting my intelligence, the anger inside me grew and my hands began to tremble.

"Really, Amanda?" I asked, tilting my head. "So, let me get this straight. Rick Kashinsky, the CCO at Corporate, flew me to Florida, put me through a rigorous interview, and spent almost three hours with me discussing my qualifications because he wants me to count erasers and desks. Is that right?"

"Yes."

"Okay—well, I'm a number cruncher and I enjoy counting so I'm still interested and am looking forward to receiving my offer letter."

After Amanda left my office, I was still trembling and had to take a few deep breaths to calm my nerves.

Another week passed and I still had not received the offer of employment for the regional position from Corporate. I did, however, receive four urgent voice messages back-to-back from Frank Adams, the racist Corporate VP of Quality Assurance, requesting that I re-email him my resume immediately.

I guess I didn't respond to his messages fast enough because after the fourth message, I also received the following urgent email:

Ebony—

Can you email me your resume right away? I lost my copy. I don't need anything else, just your resume. Send me your resume right away.

Frank Adams
Corporate Vice President of Quality Assurance

I didn't know what the heck was going on, but took Frank's frantic voice messages and email as a good sign. And after complying with his request, I was hopeful that I would receive the employment offer letter within a matter of days. But when two more weeks passed and I still had not received it, my hopes were dashed.

Now, at this point, you're probably wondering why I didn't just jump over everyone's head and contact Rick Kashinsky, the Chief

Compliance Officer at Corporate, directly to find out the status of my employment offer?

The reason is simple. One of the skills an effective leader in any organization must have is the ability to problem solve, and if I would have jumped over everyone's head at this stage of the process, it was highly likely that Rick Kashinsky would lose confidence in my ability to deal with conflict, and I wasn't willing to risk bringing in the big guns until I had enough evidence to prove my suspicions that I was being discriminated against because I was Black—again.

On February 12, 2018, Amanda Ross, the diamond-covered Chancellor of the Austin Campus, walked into my office unannounced and weirdness entered the scene once more.

"Ebony, you need to send an email to Rick Kashinsky, telling him you're not interested in the regional position.

"I never said I wasn't interested, Amanda. I said I'm very interested."

Amanda huffed and walked out of my office almost as fast as she walked in.

I'm assuming that Amanda and Travis Clayton, the National Director of Human Resources, were conspiring together to get me out of the regional position, because forty-five minutes later, Travis sent an email to all staff and faculty in the Daebrun division that made me so angry I almost screamed. The email was an internal job posting for the Regional Director of Quality Assurance and Compliance position…The same position I applied for, jumped through all kinds of hoops for, and that I was promised! And when I reviewed the job description, it was exactly the same! Nothing had changed and there was no mention of counting erasers, desks, or anything else!

Furious and on the verge of tears, I sat in my chair shaking as reality sat in that I was about to lose something else in a world that was falling apart at the speed of light. I had already lost the love of my life; mom's health was declining, and I feared it wouldn't be long before I lost her, too; and now I was losing the regional position and with it any chance I had of getting away from Dr. Gershon. But as I sat there pondering all the things I was losing or had already lost that I had no control over, I drew strength from God, realizing that I did have some control over whether I lost the regional director position. So, over the next five minutes, I typed and sent the following email to Frank Adams, the racist Corporate VP of Quality Assurance, and saved it as evidence:

Dear Frank,

On December 27, 2017, you called and informed me that Rick Kashinsky, Chief Compliance Officer, was very interested in me for the Regional Director of Quality Assurance and Compliance position and was planning to make me an offer of employment. Attached is the email I sent you that day confirming our conversation.

Today, the attached internal job posting for the same position I was promised was sent to all staff and faculty in the Daebrun division by Travis Clayton, National Director of Human Resources, and I am thoroughly confused and suspect that I'm being forced out of the position because I'm Black.

Sincerely,

Ebony Ardoin, National Director of Student Finance

The email I sent to Frank Adams must have rattled him because ten minutes later, Travis Clayton, the National Director of Human Resources, sent another email to all staff and faculty in the Daebrun division retracting the internal job posting with one sentence that read: *"The Regional Director of Quality Assurance and Compliance position is not currently open."*

The next morning as I was logging into my computer, my desk phone rang. It was Dr. Gershon.

"Ebony, I need you to stop by my office."

90

"Do you want me to bring you coffee?"

"No, just come on in."

"Sure, I'm on my way."

After locking my purse in my desk, I went to Dr. Gershon's office and immediately noticed Amanda Ross, the Chancellor of the Austin campus, sitting in front of his desk and nervously twisting her diamond ring. I knew the meeting was about the regional position and closed the door for privacy.

"Ebony, I don't understand why someone with your immense talents wants a clerk's job, counting erasers and desks."

"I enjoy counting," I said, smiling wide. "Didn't Amanda tell you?"

Dr. Gershon's cheeks turned red and he glared at me.

"I don't appreciate your flippant attitude," he sternly said. "You're *not* getting the position and it has nothing to do with your skin color. There's no way in hell I'll allow Corporate to put you or anyone with no degree in a position with oversight over educated folks with masters and doctorate degrees. No way in hell! You're not getting the position because you're not qualified, so you can stop trying to use the Black card!"

"I'm not qualified to count erasers and desks?"

Dr. Gershon's eye began to twitch as he slammed his fist on the table.

"You *will* rescind your application, Ebony. You no longer have my approval to apply."

"No—I—won't," I replied, putting emphasis on each word.

He leaned back in his chair as Amanda sat there, silent.

"Get the hell out of my office, Ebony!"

And with that I got up and left.

When I returned to my office, I sent the following email to Dr. Gershon and copied Amanda Ross as proof that I was being coerced into rescinding my candidacy for the regional position.

Dear Dr. Gershon,

Just a quick note to recap the conversation we (you, me, and Amanda Ross) had in your office a few minutes ago during which you stated the following:

1. The Regional Director of Quality Assurance and Compliance position has been reduced to a clerk's job, consisting of counting erasers and desks.

2. You no longer approve my candidacy for the position stating that I'm not qualified because I don't have a degree, even though the job description says a "degree is preferred but not required".

Additionally, you instructed me to rescind my application for the regional director position. I refused.

Please let me know if my understanding of our meeting is incorrect.

Sincerely,

Ebony Ardoin, National Director of Student Finance

Thirty minutes later, Travis Clayton, the National Director of Human Resources, reposted the Regional Director of Quality Assurance and Compliance position that I was promised. Not only did he email it internally to all staff and faculty in the Daebrun division, but this time he also posted it externally on several online job sites to recruit external candidates. And to make matters worse, the job description was exactly the same. Nothing had changed!

As I sat in my office, humiliated by what they were publicly doing to me and analyzing everything that had occurred since the day I applied for the regional director position, a lightbulb inside my head went off and it became clear that the only reason Dr. Gershon allowed me to apply for the regional director position was because he thought the risk of me being selected by Corporate to fill the position was exceptionally low.

Everything changed, though, when I informed Dr. Gershon that I was a finalist for the regional position, and he realized the risk of losing me as the National Director of Student Finance _and_ his secretarial workhorse had exponentially increased. So, he conspired with Frank Adams, the Corporate VP of Quality Assurance who was motivated by racism, and put a plan in motion to derail my promotion.

It started with Dr. Gershon and Frank Adams making similar statements to me that if things didn't work out, I could remain in student finance.

Then, after the decision was made by Rick Kashinsky to offer me the regional position, an additional interview with Danielle Kent, the Chancellor at the Temple campus, was added to the mix in hopes that requiring me to return to the Temple campus where I experienced severe racial trauma would discourage me from accepting the position.

Next, Dr. Gershon used the power and influence of his position as CEO of Daebrun to recruit Amanda Ross, the Chancellor of the Austin Campus, to misrepresent the scope of the position to me, indicating that it was the equivalent of a clerk and informing me that the position was a demotion not a promotion and my salary would be reduced by fifteen percent.

And after all of the above-mentioned acts to derail my acceptance of the regional position failed, Dr. Gershon attempted to coerce me into rescinding my candidacy.

At this point, I believed I had enough evidence to jump over everyone's head and address my concerns directly with Rick Kashinsky, the Chief Compliance Officer at Corporate. So, I sent him the following email:

Dear Rick,

On December 27, 2017, I was informed by Frank Adams, Corporate Vice President of Quality Assurance, that you had selected me to fill the Regional Director of Quality Assurance and Compliance position and that an employment offer from you would be forthcoming.

Today, after being coerced by Dr. Gershon to rescind my candidacy which I refused to do, the same regional position that I was told I would receive was posted internally and externally (see attached) and it appears that I am no longer the candidate you want to fill this position.

It was my pleasure to interview with you. Thank you again for your hospitality.

Sincerely,

Ebony Ardoin, National Director of Student Finance

Five minutes later, I received a phone call from a very confused Rick Kashinsky.

"Just got your email, Ebony. Frank told me you were no longer interested in the regional position and decided to stay in student finance," he said. "That's why the position was reposted."

"Frank lied to you. I *never* said I wasn't interested in the regional position."

Over the next thirty minutes, I explained everything that had happened starting from the day Frank informed me that Rick was going to give me an offer of employment and ending with Dr. Gershon's coercion attempt.

"This is disturbing on so many levels," Rick replied. "Looks like I have some investigative work to do. I'll be in touch."

After hanging up with Rick, I documented our telephone conversation in my Daily Log and felt a sense of relief because I knew that if anyone could get to the bottom of what was going on, it was Rick.

An hour and a half later, I received a frantic phone call from Amanda Ross, the Chancellor of the Austin campus.

"Ebony, can you please come to my office?"

"For what?"

"I just spoke with Rick at Corporate. I don't want Dr. G to know I'm talking to you."

"Okay, I'm on my way."

Ten minutes later, I arrived at Amanda's office in Building 1 where she was pacing across the floor as she nervously twisted the diamond ring on her finger. When she saw me, she motioned me to come in and quickly closed the door behind me. She was too nervous to sit and just started talking.

"I just got off the phone with Rick," she said, talking a million miles a minute. "He said you told him we forced you out of the regional position. He accused me of discrimination!"

"Is that why you called me over here, Amanda?"

"No," she quickly replied, shaking her head as tears filled the bottom of her eyes. "I didn't want Dr. G to see us. I'm not losing my job for him or anyone else."

"Okay."

"I wanted you to know—I told Rick the truth."

"What did you tell him?"

"I told him Dr. G coerced me into giving you inaccurate information about the job."

When Amanda said she confessed to Rick that Dr. Gershon coerced her into leading me astray, it was comforting in a weird sort of way because I knew that when he realized that she sold him out, he would view her as an enemy. I can't remember who said, 'the enemy of my

95

enemy is my friend', but I think it best describes how I felt about her that day, even though I still didn't trust her as far as I could throw her.

"Thank you for telling him the truth, Amanda," I replied. "The main reason I want the regional position is to get away from Dr. Gershon. I hate reporting to him, and I really hate working in Building 2."

I bet you're shaking your head right now, thinking it was dumb of me to tell Amanda how I felt about Dr. Gershon. But in my own defense, I did it because the truth was out. Amanda's lies had come to an end, and I was confident that Dr. Gershon's days as the CEO of Daebrun were numbered and that he would become another person who unexpectedly resigned for "personal reasons" within a matter of days...or so I thought.

CHAPTER 11

THE END OF LIFE

TWO WEEKS HAD PASSED SINCE AMANDA'S CONFESSION to Rick Kashinsky, the Chief Compliance Officer at Corporate, and Dr. Gershon appeared to suffer no consequences whatsoever. He was still the CEO of Daebrun; still expecting me to make his damn coffee; still requiring me to be his secretarial workhorse; and still conducting business as usual as if nothing ever happened.

And to make matters worse, the internal and external job postings for the Regional Director of Quality Assurance and Compliance position that I was promised were still active, turning me into a laughing stock on campus as rumors began to spread about my rejected candidacy. My anxiety was at an all-time high, and I kicked myself repeatedly for naively thinking that the racism I previously endured at Daebrun was a one-time thing and that I would never experience it again after I proved systemic racism the first time. And although it was tempting to quit my job, I firmly believed it was better to deal with the racist demons at Daebrun I already knew than to get a different job and be forced to deal with a new horde of demons I didn't know anything about.

But as bad as things were at work, they were even worse at home. Mom's hallucinations were becoming more frequent, and she was sleeping way more than usual because of the increased dosage of morphine needed to manage her pain.

And although she was still able to walk for short distances on her own and still had somewhat of an appetite, she was eating a lot less and losing too much weight.

As I sat at my desk drowning in a sea of tears, my cell phone rang. It was Cody.

"Babe, can we talk? I need to see you."

"Are you still married?"

"Yes, but—"

"But what?"

"But we can work this out. We can still be together and—"

I hung up. I didn't want to hear how we could sneak around and continue seeing each other. But truth be told, I missed him. I missed him so damn much. I missed the attention he gave me. I missed the contrast of his vanilla skin against mine. And more than anything, I missed the way he made passionate love to me. But I needed more from him than he was willing to give, and I was done being his side chick.

For the rest of the day, I attempted to pull myself together and rededicate myself to my career in student finance since it was clear that I was not going to get the regional position.

I finally made it home from work and was emotionally, mentally, and physically drained. And when I walked through the door and got a glimpse of Gabrielle upstairs in the kitchen cooking dinner and Aiyden downstairs watching TV without a care in the world, I was beyond grateful for my beautiful big sister because I knew that without her love and support to help me deal with the enormous amount of stress I was carrying, I probably would've snapped by now and ended up in someone's mental institution.

After eating dinner, I spent the next hour helping Aiyden with his homework and playing a few games with him. Then, I left him in Gabrielle's care so I could spend some precious time with mom.

When I walked into my room, Mom was sitting up in the bed watching TV and picking at the food on her plate.

"Hey honey," she said with a faint smile. "How was ya' day?"

98

"Long, I'm glad to be home. You feeling okay, mom?"

I walked over and kissed her on the cheek.

"I'm doin' fine. I tried to read my Bible, but my eyes are a little blurry."

I grabbed mom's Bible from the top of the nightstand.

"Want me to read your favorite chapter?"

Mom smiled wide.

"Yes honey, that'll be just fine."

I opened mom's Bible and turned to Psalms 118:24.

"This *is* the day the Lord has made," I read. "We will rejoice and be glad in it."

Mom smiled and put her plate down on the nightstand as I continued reading to her for the next thirty minutes.

A few minutes later, Gabrielle came in to collect mom's plate and kiss her goodnight.

"Gabby," Mom said. "Lay with me for a minute."

As Gabrielle climbed into bed and sat up next to mom, I put her Bible back down on the nightstand. Then Mom grabbed one of each of our hands.

"Gabby. Eb," Mom said, looking back and forth between us. "You girls are my rock, my joy, and my strength. I love you both so much."

Gabrielle and I started crying instantly.

"We love you, too, mom," Gabrielle said, trying to choke back her tears.

"We love you so much," I cried. "We've been the three musketeers for as long as I can remember."

Mom smiled as a river of tears rolled down her cheeks.

"I want you to know it's been my greatest privilege and honor to be your mom. And when I leave, don't be sad. The Apostle Paul said to be absent from the body is to be present with the Lord. That means the

99

minute I leave this decaying body I'll be right there with Jesus, and I'll still be me. I'll still be alive, and I'll still be your mom. So never lose your faith in Jesus, girls, so we can be together again. Understand?"

We both acknowledged our understanding and for the next five minutes we held Mom tight and got lost in an ocean of emotions.

Gabrielle kissed Mom goodnight and left to help Aiyden get ready for bed. I was too tired to take a shower, so I went into the bathroom and put on my pajamas. By the time I finished five minutes later, Mom was already sound asleep.

I was emotionally, mentally, and physically exhausted, so I climbed into bed and fell asleep within minutes of my head hitting the pillow.

Suddenly, Mom screamed.

"I'll kill ya'! Get the hell out of our house!"

I abruptly woke up terrified and violently shaking as Mom jumped out of bed with a burst of energy and took off down the hall.

I jumped out of bed and went after her.

"I'll kill ya'!" Mom continued screaming. "Where's my gun?"

"Mom," Gabby said, stopping her in the living room and trying to calm her down. "Everything's okay."

Mom's breathing was labored.

"Get my gun in case they come back," she insisted.

"Okay, mom," Gabrielle calmly said. "You go with Eb back to bed, okay?"

I gently wrapped my arm around mom's shoulder and walked with her down the hallway back to my room. Then I tucked her in, kissed her on the forehead, and climbed back into bed on the other side.

My body was wired and still shaking from mom's terrifying outburst, but I managed to fall back asleep from pure exhaustion.

Suddenly, Mom sat up in the bed.

"You hear that, Eb?"

I opened my now bloodshot eyes wide.

"Hear what, mom?"

"That music, Eb. That beautiful music."

Mom started swaying to and fro as she listened to music that only she could hear.

For the next few hours, it was more of the same. Every time I fell asleep even for a minute, Mom either screamed, scaring the crap out of me, laughed at things that only she could see, swayed to music that only she could hear, or jumped out of bed to chase thieves. I was at my wits end and on the verge of collapsing from pure exhaustion.

Finally, after tucking Mom back into bed for the fourth or fifth time, her head sank into the pillow, and she fell asleep, and I was so grateful to God.

I was a nervous wreck by this point and was worried that Mom might have another episode so I climbed into bed and laid on my side facing her to make sure I could immediately see her when I open my eyes. Things were quiet for the next few hours as Mom peacefully slept, and I finally relaxed enough to fall into a deep sleep.

But that didn't last long, as a few hours later, an eerie feeling came over me and I was compelled to open my eyes. Slowly, I blinked and allowed my eyes to adjust to the darkness, and to my surprise, found myself staring into Mom's blank wide-open eyes, as drool slid from the side of her mouth onto her pillow. She wasn't blinking. She didn't even appear to be breathing.

She just stared at me, as I laid there frozen and scared beyond belief. "Are...you...scared?" She asked, still staring at me with wide non-blinking eyes.

"Not until this very moment," I responded, too afraid to blink or even move. Then, before I knew it, I let out a blood curdling scream.

"Gabby!" I yelled, crying between words. "Mom's scaring me!"

Gabby and Aiyden ran into my room, where I was crying hysterically.

When Gabby saw mom's condition, she immediately called the hospice nurse and mom's pastor. Mom's pulse was weak, and by the time the hospice nurse arrived, she was no longer able to form words, but her hearing seemed to be intact as Aiyden, Gabrielle, and I showered her with love, hugs, and kisses. An hour later, Mom's physical life ended, and we all held hands as Mom's Pastor prayed over her.

I thought I was handling Mom's passing relatively well. But when Gabrielle tried to close Mom's eyes, and they opened back up, I lost it.

"Gabby! Mom's alive! She's alive!" I screamed.

And when the coroner arrived shortly thereafter, I really lost it.

"No, Gabby! No!" I pleaded. "Don't let them take Mom away! Mom's sleeping! She's sleeping!"

Gabby cried her eyes out as I begged her to do something.

"Please! Mom's alive! She's alive!"

I climbed into my bed, laid my head on Mom's shoulder, and held on to her for dear life until I fainted.

When I came to, Mom was gone, and the house was eerily still. All I could hear was the sound of my alarm clock ticking the minutes away. And as I watched Gabrielle and Aiyden laying in Mom's bed next to me, I was heartbroken.

I took a sip from the glass of water that Gabrielle lovingly put on the nightstand for me and laid back on the pillow as tear after tear streamed down my face. Then, I closed my eyes and sought help from our Father who is in Heaven.

"Father God…it's me…Ebony. You already know mom's life on earth ended today. But the Apostle Paul said to be absent from the body is to be present with the Lord and I just want you to know that my mind knows mom's with Jesus. But my heart hurts. It hurts so bad. And so I pray that you help my heart catch up with my mind so I can be the same rock for Gabrielle that she's been for me my entire life and I can be there for Aiyden to help him get through this tough time. In Jesus, holy, mighty, and beautiful name I pray. Amen."

I knew it was a simple prayer. But I also knew that God heard my prayer no matter how simple it was.

102

After praying, I stared at the ceiling and focused on the ticking sound of the alarm clock until my eyes became heavy and I began to fall asleep. Now, I don't know exactly how long after I fell asleep that I began to dream, all I know is that in my dream I was in my pajamas pulling weeds in my backyard under the starlit sky. For hours, I frantically pulled those weeds, big ones, and little ones, until my fingers cramped and, in some cases, bled. I cried out to God and fell to the ground, writhing in agony from emotional pain, and weeping as ants and other creatures of the night crawled across my skin.

Then, I looked up and saw a star falling from the sky directly above me. I watched for a while expecting the star to burn up in the atmosphere but, for some reason, it didn't. It kept falling and as it got closer, I squinted to protect my eyes from the brilliant light.

I continued laying on the ground and watching the star fall until it was literally hovering over me. And that's when I saw mom, floating in the middle of that radiant light, as beautiful as ever. Her long silky black hair had returned and was flowing in the wind. Her eyes were as green as emeralds and full of love. Her skin shimmered like glittering gold. And she was wearing a radiant white gown that swayed in the wind.

Mom didn't say a word, but the smile on her face and the love in her eyes said it all. Mom was still alive! She still knew me! She could see me! And she knew how to find me!

A few minutes later, she disappeared into a light that was as bright as the sun, and I knew at that moment that everything was going to be okay. When Mom's physical life ended, her spiritual life with Jesus began and she was happy.

When I awoke, I shared the dream I had with Gabrielle and Aiyden which gave them both a great deal of comfort. And over the next few days, we made the arrangements to give Mom the homegoing celebration she so richly deserved and made sure we honored her request to be buried wearing the white suit and hat she wore to the Pastor's anniversary.

Then, we chartered a private jet, flew with Mom to Shreveport, Louisiana, and gave her a homegoing celebration of life that was worthy of her magnificence, starting with the golden casket that housed her physical body and ending with the horse drawn carriage that carried her to her final resting place in the cemetery where her Mom was also buried.

Two weeks later, I returned to work, and as I sat down to begin my day, my desk phone rang. It was Amanda Ross, the Chancellor of the Austin campus.

"Ebony, I'm so sorry to hear about your mom," she said. "I lost my Mom to lung cancer eighteen years ago. I know how hard it is."

"Thanks, Amanda. I appreciate that."

"I have some exciting news that I hope will make your day. Frank told Dr. G that Corporate's going to offer you the regional director position today!"

"Really? That's great news!"

"Here's the thing, though. Dr. G really doesn't want to lose you to Corporate, so he's authorized me to offer you a promotion, too."

"Seriously?"

"Seriously. So, this call is my verbal offer of employment to you for a promotion to Sr. Director of Academic and Registrar Operations, which will be effective immediately *if you agree to decline the regional position.*"

When Amanda told me that Frank Adams told Dr. Gershon that Corporate was going to offer me the regional position that day, it confirmed my suspicions that Frank, the racist piece of shit at Corporate, had been conspiring with Dr. Gershon the whole time. And even though I believed that Frank Adams' motives for keeping me out of the regional position were purely racist, I knew Dr. Gershon wasn't worried about losing me to Corporate any more than he was worried about the man in the moon.

I knew what he was really worried about were my analytical skills being used by Corporate in a compliance capacity at his colleges. You see, as the regional director of quality assurance and compliance with oversight over *all departments* at the Austin and Temple campuses, I would have access to everything—all reports, all data, all financial records, and all information and he knew that if there were any shady goings-on at Daebrun that he didn't want Corporate to know about, I'd find them with that level of access.

"If you accept my promotion," Amanda continued. "You'll report directly to me and receive a ten percent salary increase; your office will be moved to Building 1 away from Dr. G which is something I know you want; you'll be expanding your knowledge of higher education which is the professional growth you said you wanted; and you'll also be eligible for a twenty percent annual incentive program bonus."

"Hmm, that's quite an offer Amanda," I replied. "Before I accept, I want to receive the offer of employment from Corporate I was promised so that I can do a comparison. And one more thing, if I accept your offer, I want my sister, Gabrielle, to be eligible to receive tuition reimbursement since I'm not married and don't have any children who are old enough to use it."

"Fair enough, I'll let Dr. G know."

I returned to my office and immediately sent Amanda Ross and email confirming everything she told me as evidence. Three hours later, I received a call from Doug Harper, the Corporate Director of Human Resources who replaced Tiffany Mathers. Tiffany Mathers was the Corporate HR woman I reported the discrimination I was enduring at the Temple campus to and whose lack of action caused me to suffer retaliation.

"Morning Ebony, this is Doug Harper, Corporate Director of HR."

"Good morning, Doug."

"I'm calling to extend a verbal employment offer to you for the Regional Director of Quality Assurance and Compliance position."

"Okay, great."

"Because of your current position and salary as National Director, this position will be a lateral move with no salary increase."

"Okay, I'll need twenty-four hours to consider it."

After hanging up, I sent an email to Doug Harper confirming our conversation as evidence.

Thirty minutes later, I called Amanda Ross and informed her that I accepted the promotion she offered me to Sr. Director of Academic and Registrar Operations.

Now, I'm sure you're probably wondering why I accepted her position knowing that Dr. Gershon was the mastermind behind it and was the King Cobra in the sea of racist snakes I was surrounded by at Daebrun. The reason is simple.

I knew that there were racists at Corporate—thanks to Frank Adams,—but what I didn't know was how many of them there were or what they were capable of. And like I already said, I believed it was better to deal with the racist demons at Daebrun I already knew than to work for Corporate and be forced to deal with a new horde of demons I didn't know anything about...or so I thought.

CHAPTER 12

THE END OF CAREER

AN HOUR AFTER I VERBALLY ACCEPTED THE SR. Director of Education and Registrar Operations promotion, Travis emailed the following organizational announcement to all staff and faculty at the Austin campus making my promotion official.

It is with great pleasure that I announce the promotion of Ebony Ardoin to Sr. Director of Education and Registrar Operations. Ebony has been an integral part of our success in Student Finance and brings a wealth of knowledge and skills to this new position. I am confident she will approach this new role with the same commitment to quality and ask you to join me in congratulating her.

Travis Clayton

National Director of Human Resources

Immediately after receiving the announcement, I called Doug Harper, the Corporate Director of Human Resources, as well as Rick Kashinsky, the Chief Compliance Officer at Corporate, and declined the offer of employment for the Regional Director of Quality Assurance and Compliance position. The next day, my career in student finance officially ended, and after my office was relocated to the Education department in Building 1, I assumed the role of Sr. Director of Education and Registrar Operations. As was typical for every position I'd held at Daebrun thus far, I was not given a fair transition and received just one day of subpar training from my predecessor, while also assuming responsibility for six employees.

My employees, who were responsible for registering students, maintaining education records, scheduling classrooms, planning graduation ceremonies, entering grades into the student database, and monitoring satisfactory academic progress were burnt out and frustrated, and their morale was so low they could barely function. In short, they *hated* their jobs. And as I began reviewing the audit findings that seemed to increase year after year, I began to understand the reason Dr. Gershon decided to put me in *this* department out of all the possible departments he could have chosen.

This department was running worse than the student finance department at the Temple campus before I began managing it. For starters, there was no reliable system in place to schedule classrooms; everything was done manually, which, as you can imagine, was not an effective way to assign classrooms to courses being offered and resulted in numerous double bookings every single semester, causing extreme frustration between students and faculty alike.

And as if double-booked classrooms weren't bad enough, the faculty and Deans had absolutely no respect for my predecessor or the team I inherited. Many of them had an air of superiority about them, much like the bigwigs in Building 2, and only cared about standing in front of their classrooms teaching students. They had no desire to complete the administrative functions associated with their positions.

So, because they didn't see the value in doing things like turning in grades earned on time at the end of each semester, many of them disregarded deadlines and were consistently late which had a massive ripple effect. Their inability to turn in grades in a timely matter resulted in a delay in my department's ability to post grades and check that satisfactory academic progress was being met for every student, which resulted in a delay in the Student Finance Office's ability to request federal funds for students, which then resulted in a delay to the stipend checks students were expecting to receive to pay their bills. So, every semester end, hundreds of angry students took out their frustrations on the employees in the Student Finance Office, who in turn took out *their* frustrations on my department, and my department took out their frustrations on the faculty. It was a hot mess.

But it gets worse because even the way that students registered for upcoming classes and how academic records were maintained were a disaster. Students were required to manually fill out registration slips in ink, which required my team to manually enter them into the student database—a time waster that also created a lot of errors. And physical files for each student, containing hard copies of important documents were maintained at offsite storage facilities, which was costly and created a perfect storm for files to be lost and for our department to receive multiple audit findings per year.

But you know me, I had computer skills that were strong and diversified. So, over the next four months, I feverishly worked hard at automating and streamlining the processes that were manually being done. For starters, scanners were purchased for everyone on my team and all physical files were converted to electronic files, making significant improvements in file location and efficiency. And because the electronic files were backed up, off-site storage costs and lost documents became a thing of the past.

I also worked with the new IT Director who replaced Cody after he resigned and implemented a registration add-on for students to access via their student portal so students could electronically register for upcoming courses online themselves.

But one of the biggest accomplishments I made was designing a robust electronic room scheduling system, so students and faculty alike would know which classrooms their courses were assigned to ahead of time—something they never knew in the past until the first day of classes.

Because of the accuracy of the room scheduling system I designed, double-booked classrooms also became a thing of the past and my team and Amanda Ross, the Chancellor of the Austin campus, were beyond thrilled.

But not everyone at the Austin campus was singing my praises. Many of the faculty members and Deans hated me because I started holding them accountable for posting grades on time. I started sending out daily emails to all faculty reminding them of the approaching deadline for submitting grades to my team and copied the leaders of *every* department on the email, including Amanda Ross, the Chancellor of the Austin campus, and Amy Gray, the new CEO of the Daebrun division who replaced Dr. Gershon after he unexpectedly resigned for personal reasons.

And immediately after the deadline passed, I would send a follow-up email to the entire faculty, as well as the leaders in the other departments, listing the names of the faculty members whose grades were not received on time. And as faculty quickly learned that I wasn't the one to mess with, we started receiving their grades on time and everything in my department was finally running smoothly.

My career as the Sr. Director of Education and Registrar Operations continued to flourish through the rest of 2018. And even though I was hated by more than half of the faculty members and Deans— who, by the way were all White—I didn't let it discourage me.

That is, until the morning of January 2, 2019, right after I returned to work from the New Year's Day holiday. I had just gotten to work, when Karen Jasper, the Corporate Vice President of Education and Registrar Operations, showed up at my door, wearing a gray skirt suit with a white pearl necklace. She was a full-figured woman in her mid-thirties with fair skin, light blue eyes that appeared ice cold, and shoulder length red hair that looked brittle and dry and although I talked with her numerous times on conference calls during the last four months, this was my first time meeting her in person.

"Ebony, sorry to just pop in," she said with a thick accent. "Do you have a minute?"

"Sure, come on in."

She walked in, closed the door behind her, and sat down in front of my desk.

"We're getting a lot of complaints about you at Corporate from people in the education department—and not just faculty," she said.

"People who have a very negative opinion about you and your style of management. They say that your methods are intolerable and that you seem to be on some kind of power trip."

"Okay."

"So, to be quite frank with you," she continued. "I've been watching you for a while and I've noticed something different. You may be a little demanding, but you've created great processed and imposed much needed deadlines. And you're an expert when it comes to communicating what you're doing."

"Thank you. That's great to hear. I know change isn't always easy, but it was needed."

"You're right. And because of your stellar management, efficiency and productivity have dramatically improved and we've had less internal audit findings."

"That's great. I'm glad you're pleased."

"I am pleased," she said before popping a mint into her mouth. "And that's why I'm considering you for the position of Assistant Vice President of Education and Registrar Operations for the entire Daebrun division of course."

"Oh wow, that's amazing!"

Karen went on to say that my role as the Assistant VP would be to develop processes and procedures for all campuses in the Daebrun division, provide training, and ensure that all processes were aligned and being followed at all campuses. She also stated that in my new role, each campus Director of Education and Registrar Operations would have a dotted line reporting relationship with me, and that I would continue reporting to Amanda Ross, the Chancellor of the Austin campus, but that I would *also* have a dotted line reporting relationship to her.

She also said she wanted to see me conducting bi-weekly meetings with the campus directors to discuss issues, brainstorm ideas, provide training, and talk about any other items that were deemed necessary. She said the official announcement of my new role, if I accepted, would be made in early February. It was the opportunity of a lifetime!

"I'd like to give you a test run, you know, to test your skills with plans to extend a formal offer to you during the first week in February. How does that sound?"

"Sounds great! I cannot thank you enough for this opportunity."

After the meeting ended, I sent Karen an email confirming everything she said as evidence and then went to Amanda Ross' office.

"Amanda, you'll never guess in a million years what just happened!"

"You were offered the Assistant VP position," she said with a smile. "Congratulations, that's great. It's even greater that you don't have to relocate to Corporate because if you accept, you'll stay right here which makes me happy."

The next day during the campus management meeting, where I was the only Black person in a leadership position, Amanda announced my appointment to Assistant VP of Education and Registrar Operations and the reactions were mixed. Some people congratulated me, while others— including all of the Deans—didn't say a single word.

Later that afternoon, Jeff Jones, a Black faculty member who was also my friend, stopped by my office. Jeff was a handsome man in his early fifties who taught criminal justice and served on the police force for fifteen years. He was a tall muscular man with dark chocolate skin, black buzz cut hair, hazel eyes that looked like polished stones, and muscular legs I'm sure could choke a lion.

"Ebony! Just heard about your promotion! Congratulations!"

"Thanks, Jeff. I'm excited!"

"I'm relieved. I thought you were in some kind of trouble when I saw that White woman meeting with all those White folks that can't stand you."

"Who was she meeting with?"

Jeff continued, saying that Karen met with all the Deans, all the Chairs, and many members of faculty and seemed to be gathering information about me.

"She was probably making sure I was the right fit for the position before she met with me," I replied.

112

Over the next thirty days, Karen added a ton of additional work to my plate to "test" my skills for the VP position. I was conducting weekly conference calls with the Directors of Education and Registrar Operations at all campuses in the Daebrun division, writing proposals to increase the use of technology in the education departments at all campuses, providing written updates to the Chancellors at all campuses on education initiatives accomplished for the division under my leadership, as well as providing training to the education and registrar operations teams at all campuses.

I was also required to represent the Daebrun division during a federal audit and prepared numerous standard operating procedures for all campuses. My workload quadrupled to the point that I was working well over eighty hours a week. And as hard as it was, I kept up with the demand because I was determined to show her I was qualified for the position.

On February 4, 2019, my desk phone rang. It was Karen Jasper, the Corporate Vice President of Education and Registrar Operations.

"Ebony, great news! Corporate approved our use of your technology proposal!"

"That's wonderful news, I'm glad to hear it!"

"Now, we'll need to meet with the Chancellors to discuss the roll out."

"Before we do that, Karen, we need to discuss the employment offer for the VP position. Where are we with that? It's been thirty days."

"Let me check with HR, I'll get back to you."

Two days later, when I had not received a phone call back from Karen to provide me with a status update, I sent her the following email:

Karen,

This email is to follow up on the employment offer for the Assistant Vice President of Education and Registrar Operations position you said would be

---

extended to me during our meeting on January 2, 2019. It has been more than thirty days since I assumed responsibility for duties associated with this position and I have yet to receive the employment offer.

Please provide me with a status update as soon as possible.

Sincerely,

Ebony Ardoin, Sr. Director of Education and Registrar Operations

Five minutes after sending my email, my desk phone rang. It was Karen.

"Ebony, I'm working on your offer of employment, so I need you to be patient. We're working out the details so give us a little time, okay?"

"Sure, thanks for the update."

It was at this time that I realized that I was being yanked around again, just as they had done with the first position I was told I was going to get before I was sabotaged by racists.

Forty-five more days went by and not only had I not received the employment offer, but I was still doing all of the work associated with the VP position and working well over eighty hours a week. Until finally, Karen called me.

"Hi, Ebony. I have an update on the position. Unfortunately, we have to rescind our offer. I didn't realize that you don't have a bachelor's degree, which is something the VP position requires."

"Of course you didn't," I said. "And how convenient that this realization came after three months of *testing* my competence and skills for the role—of which, you have done nothing but sing my praises."

With nothing left to say, and Karen unable to justify why, out of the blue, my education became a major factor in their decision, I realized there was no way I could ever continue working at this place. I was done with racists at Daebrun and I was done with racists at Corporate. I had reached the end of a tumultuous, exhausting, and humiliating journey, and was emotionally spent, with nothing left to give them, and no hope that I would ever be able to step into my full potential.

Between the stress of losing Mom and having to maintain so much just to be continually shot down from racist gatekeepers, it was too much. And so I resigned to keep my sanity. I paid the ultimate price for being Black in Corporate America, as I was forced out of multiple opportunities and suffered so much racial trauma—that, honestly, I will probably never recover from—and had no other option left but to quit and lose everything I'd worked to achieve at that company.

But fortunately, I still had enough money from my settlement to tide us over for a little while after Gabrielle, Aiyden and I moved to Maryland for a fresh start, and I *knew* that when I was ready to return to Corporate America, my career future would be lightyears better than my career past and I would never experience racism in the workplace again. Because, after all, lightning never strikes three times...or so I thought.

A NOTE FROM THE AUTHORS

"Thank you for reading Hush Money. Please post a review on Amazon to inspire others to read it. Amazon reviews are vital to our success as self-published authors, and we appreciate your love and support."

- Jacquie, Deborah, & Delilah

Made in the USA
Las Vegas, NV
08 February 2022